Adam Collins: One of Mission Creek's bravest firefighters, he risks his life for a living. But saving little Jake Anderson from the blazing country club touches him to the very core. Does Adam dare lose his heart to both the little boy and his beautiful, vivacious doctor?

Dr. Tracy Walker: The dedicated pediatric burn specialist works her magic to ease Jake's pain. Unable to have children of her own, she yearns for a little boy like Jake. Can she find room in her life for a certain strong but silent firefighter, as well?

Jake Anderson: The five-year-old boy knows who's responsible for the Lone Star Country Club bombing but is mute from the shock of losing his parents in the blast. Will Tracy and Adam be able to keep him safe till he's able to reveal the truth?

Police Chief Benjamin Stone: Horrified to discover that bombers have attacked *his* town, he's put the Mission Creek police on full alert. Will he uncover the identity of the attackers and bring them to justice before it's too late?

Dear Reader,

Valentine's Day is here, a time for sweet indulgences. RITA Award-winning author Merline Lovelace is happy to oblige as she revisits her popular CODE NAME: DANGER miniseries. In *Hot as Ice*, a frozen Cold War-era pilot is thawed out by beautiful scientist Diana Remington, who soon finds herself taking her work home with her.

ROMANCING THE CROWN continues with *The Princess and the Mercenary*, by RITA Award winner Marilyn Pappano. Mercenary Tyler Ramsey reluctantly agrees to guard Princess Anna Sebastiani as she searches for her missing brother, but who will protect Princess Anna's heart from Tyler? In Linda Randall Wisdom's *Small-Town Secrets*, a young widow—and detective—tries to solve a string of murders with the help of a handsome reporter. The long-awaited LONE STAR COUNTRY CLUB series gets its start with Marie Ferrarella's *Once a Father*. A bomb has ripped apart the Club, and only a young boy rescued from the wreckage knows the identity of the bombers. The child's savior, firefighter Adam Collins, and his doctor, Tracy Walker, have taken the child into protective custody—where they will fight danger from outside and attraction from within. RaeAnne Thayne begins her OUTLAW HARTES series with *The Valentine Two-Step*. Watch as two matchmaking little girls turn their schemes on their unsuspecting single parents. And in Nancy Morse's *Panther on the Prowl*, a temporarily blinded woman seeks shelter—and finds much more—in the arms of a mysterious stranger.

Enjoy them all, and come back next month, because the excitement never ends in Silhouette Intimate Moments.

Yours,

Leslie. J. Wainger
Executive Senior Editor

Please address questions and book requests to:
Silhouette Reader Service
U.S.: 3010 Walden Ave., P.O. Box 1325, Buffalo, NY 14269
Canadian: P.O. Box 609, Fort Erie, Ont. L2A 5X3

Once a Father
MARIE FERRARELLA

Silhouette®

INTIMATE MOMENTS™

Published by Silhouette Books

America's Publisher of Contemporary Romance

Special thanks and acknowledgment are given
to Marie Ferrarella for her contribution
to the LONE STAR COUNTRY CLUB series.

 SILHOUETTE BOOKS

ISBN 0-373-27202-2

ONCE A FATHER

Visit Silhouette at www.eHarlequin.com

Printed in U.S.A.

Books by Marie Ferrarella in Miniseries

MARIE FERRARELLA

earned a master's degree in Shakespearean comedy and, perhaps as a result, her writing is distinguished by humor and natural dialogue. This RITA Award-winning author's goal is to entertain and to make people laugh and feel good. She has written over one hundred books for Silhouette, some under the name Marie Nicole. Her romances are beloved by fans worldwide and have been translated into Spanish, Italian, German, Russian, Polish, Japanese and Korean.

To
Maggie Price
&
Beverly Bird,
who brought new meaning
to the word
precision.
My hat
is
off
to you both.

Prologue

Mulrooney was droning on endlessly. It was obviously that the newly hired policeman had absolutely no idea what the word succinct meant. But for once, Chief Ben Stone of the Mission Creek police department didn't mind being subjected to the endless rhetoric as the much younger man was describing a recent, utterly trivial incident that had occurred in town.

He wasn't listening anyway.

The late morning Texas sun filled the office, highlighting the dust and cobwebs that the night janitorial staff had missed. Ben's dark blue eyes stealthily shifted to the watch on his wrist just beneath the cuff of his navy blue uniform. A vague hint of a smile teased the corners of his ordinarily downturned mouth as he noted the hour.

Almost time.

* * *

"Can't understand why a man who can look death in the face and spit in its eye would want to waste his time knocking around a little white ball along some stubby green grass."

Completely mystified by the attraction of the game, Luke Callaghan shook his dark head as he watched the tall, rangy silver-haired man who he respected more than any living being on the face of the earth take careful measure before making his shot. Though it was the game of choice for the people who populated the upper-crust world he lived in, Luke only played because his best friends found the game so intriguing. As for him, he could abandon the game in a heartbeat. His score reflected as much.

Leaning on his club in what could only be termed an indolent pose, Spence Harrison, the local district attorney, teased, his tongue in his cheek. "No mystery, Luke. Comes a time when a man just has to lay down the saber and do what he can to occupy his mind."

Commander Phil Westin grinned at the men he'd both led and saved when they had been part of his Marine platoon in the Gulf War. The expression softened a face that was all planes and angles, ordinarily arousing fear in the hearts of his enemies.

Lack of activity had never been a problem for Westin and he ignored Spence's good-natured jibe. "I already told you, Luke, golf relaxes me."

Keenly aware of his score and not one who enjoyed not excelling at everything he tried, Luke frowned. "Well, it frustrates the hell out of me."

Spence glanced over his friend's shoulder at the scorecard. "I can see why."

"That's because your hand-eye coordination is shot to hell," Flynt Carson kidded Luke. The country club where they were playing had originally been co-founded by his great-grandfather Jace in 1923, on land he had carved out of his ranch and donated. The other half had come from the Wainwrights, who the Carsons no longer had any dealings with for what all felt were excellent reasons. "Thank God you did better with a rifle in your hands than you do with a golf club."

Tyler Murdoch, the fifth man on the team, raised his club like a sword. Taking his cue, Luke raised his and crossed it over Tyler's. The latter gave a few thrusts and parries, which Tyler countered.

"Anything can be a weapon," Luke quipped to Tyler, "in the right person's hands."

"Boys, boys, play nice," Westin laughed. The serious nature behind the impromptu gathering blended into the laughter, making it fade. It was time he told them why he'd asked for this get-together. "Besides, this is probably the last time I'm going to be seeing you for a while and I'd like to take away an image of you overgrown Boy Scouts doing something other than clowning around."

There was a great deal of affection between them that went beyond their time together in the war. They, along with the one missing, estranged member of their former group, had all attended Virginia Military Institute, then joined the 14th Marines after graduation. The Gulf War had seen them taken prisoner and required them to demonstrate exemplary bravery under fire and extreme conditions. Though none talked about it, each man would have gone to hell and back for the others in the group.

Some of them felt they had.

"Okay, I've had it with this country club facade." Unlike Luke and Flynt, an endless supply of money had never been Tyler's problem while he was growing up. He turned to Westin. "C'mon, Commander, straight out, tell us. Why'd you call us together? What's this big mystery you're keeping from us?"

Phil slid his club into his bag and debated over which club to use for the shot. He appeared unruffled, but his mind wasn't on anything so trivial as the right club to use. "No big mystery, just don't want it advertised just yet." Taking a club out, he turned to look at the others. He needed them to know this. In case there came a time when he had to call upon them for help. "I'm being sent to Central America to see if maybe I can get a handle on how to bring down that new drug czar. Calls himself El Jefe." He smiled thinly. "No ego problem there."

Though their lives had taken them in different directions since the time they served together, the men were all up on the rumors that the newest drug route bringing illegal fare into the U.S. was passing directly through their part of the country. Maybe even through Mission Creek itself, though none of them liked to think that.

"Why you?" Luke wondered if Westin, like himself, was a secret agent. Wouldn't that have been a hoot? Two of them in one small, tight circle, each not knowing about the other.

A steely grin curved Westin's strong mouth. "Haven't you heard? They always pick the best man for the job." The hell with the game, he decided. He wanted to sit and hoist a few beers with these men before he disappeared into the jungle for who knew how long. "I've got reservations for us at the Men's Grill." He glanced at his watch. The reservation was for eleven. It was five minutes past that now. "It's already getting late. Let's go there and I'll tell you all about it. Might be something to pass along to your grandkids if you boys can ever find yourself four good women whose standards aren't too high."

Luke gladly tossed his golf club into his bag. "I'm ready to call it a game."

Eschewing carts and caddies, each man carried his own bag, just as they had once carried their own fifty-pound backpacks through a foreign land.

But as they turned toward the sprawling four-story brick complex known as the Lone Star Country Club where the Men's Grill was housed, an explosion suddenly resounded, shattering the calm of a perfect morning.

Flames belched out, infecting the horizon with smoke as the men were sent tumbling pell-mell to the ground, their golf clubs scattered all around them like so many sticks emptied out of one giant bag.

Chapter 1

"I'm not a baby, Mom. I'm old enough to go to the bathroom myself," Jake Anderson insisted. Rocking on the toes of the brand-new pair of shoes his mother had made him wear today, the boy who was five, hovering anxiously on the cusp of being six, looked to his father for backup. "Right, Dad?"

Daniel Anderson smiled affectionately at his only son. With his blond hair and fair coloring, the boy was the spitting image of his mother. The thought crossed Daniel's mind that his own mother had been right. They did grow up so fast.

"He is five, you know, Meg."

"Almost six," Jake piped up.

Margaret Anderson sighed, knowing she was being overly protective. But it was still difficult for her not to think of Jake as her little boy and as such, she didn't really want him to go wandering off on his

own, even though this was the Lone Star Country
Club, where only the best people came to pass the
time.

As if reading her mind, her husband added, "And
after all, this is the Lone Star Country Club, Meg.
Nothing bad ever happens here. Best place in the
world to start letting Jake be his own person."

Assaulted on both sides, Meg had no choice but to
relent. "I suppose." As he was about to run off, she
caught her son's hand. He looked at her, obviously
trying to curb his impatience. "Just to the men's room
and back, Jake. Don't go wandering off and don't
dawdle."

"Yes, ma'am," Jake mumbled dutifully.

Daniel made a show of checking his pockets. Not
finding what he was looking for, he snapped his fingers. "And me without my compass. Think you can
get there and back before nightfall, son?"

Jake laughed as his father ruffled his hair.

Meg took the teasing at her expense in stride. "All
right, you two." She looked at Daniel. "He's still my
little boy." She curbed the impulse to hug Jake,
knowing that displays of affection in public embarrassed him. "I'm entitled. Go now, before they bring
your dessert and it melts." She shooed her son off
and then raised her coffee cup to her lips.

Trying not to run, Jake quickly made his way
through the dining hall, afraid his mother would find
some reason to call him back. He felt like one of the
big boys now, off on his own.

In the hall, he paused, trying to remember which
direction to take to get to the men's room. He'd been

there several times with his father, but he'd never paid much attention. The long hallways all looked alike. Stubbornly, he refused to go back and ask his parents for directions, knowing that his mother would take the opportunity to come with him as she showed him the way.

Hesitating, Jake made his choice and turned to his right. He saw the green-and-white sign all the way at the end of the corridor. It said Rest Rooms. That was grown-up talk for bathrooms.

Hurrying, he passed a partially opened door. The sign across it had words he hadn't learned how to read yet. The sound of urgent voices aroused his natural curiosity and he peered inside.

What he saw was a partially darkened room filled with what looked to be a hundred television sets, all tuned to boring programs that had nothing but rooms on them. There was a single, sharp beam of light coming in from another opened door. It was on the other end of the room, to the left and the door was opened to the outside.

He thought he saw a truck and two men, each dragging a big, fat sack from the room to the door. They looked like the sack that Santa Claus had brought his toys in just last month, except that these were green. He wondered if there were toys in these sacks and if the men he saw were Santa's helpers.

One of the men looked sharply at him.

"Hey, you, kid!"

Jake jumped back, afraid that the man would tell his parents that he'd strayed. Or worse, that he'd tell

Santa and he wouldn't get any presents next Christmas.

Spinning on his heel, he ran back toward the Grill, forgetting all about his maiden solo voyage to the bathroom.

Halfway back to the dining area, he heard a big bang coming from that area at almost the same time he went flying off his feet.

His head hit the floor just as bursts of light registered in his brain.

Everything went black.

Bonnie Brannigan wasn't aware of wringing her hands, even though the action moved the large engagement ring on her hand to and fro and made her overly burdened charm bracelet jingle with each movement.

Nor did she realize that her platinum blond hair, usually so carefully and artfully arranged in a hairstyle that had been dear to her heart since her teens some forty years ago, had sunk several degrees south of its rightful position atop her head. She was far too upset to notice anything but the flames shooting out from what had once been the Men's Grill. It was clear that the restaurant and the billiards room next to it were lost. She prayed that the firemen she was watching so intently could contain the fire to this section.

What if they couldn't? The whole club was in jeopardy.

As manager of the popular Lone Star Country Club these past few years, she'd been inside her office reviewing last month's profits when the explosion had thrown her from her chair. Momentarily disoriented, the acrid smell of smoke reached her nose just as her ears were clearing of the deafening noise.

Stumbling out into the hallway, she'd been accosted by flames. One of the busboys had grabbed her hand, all but dragging her out of the building. In retrospect, he'd probably saved her life. She wasn't even sure which young man it had been.

It seemed too incredible for words.

Well clear of the building, she stood shivering beneath a coat someone had thrown on her shoulders, fighting off the tightening grasp of shock. Her eyes stung, whether from smoke or grief she wasn't altogether sure, and a tear trickled down her sooty cheek as she surveyed the damage that had been done. A panicked feeling was taking over the pit of her stomach.

Dressed in the pink colors she tended to favor, Bonnie stood out like a petite, colorful focal point amid the destruction that came in the wake of the explosion.

Her mind struggled to understand.

Was this some horrible accident, or deliberate? Who could have done this?

Noise, hoses and smoke seemed to be all around her. Right in front of her, yellow-jacketed firefighters were attempting to tame the flames.

"Nothing like this has ever happened here before," she said more to herself than to the powerfully built man standing beside her.

"Yeah, bet old Peter Wainwright and Jace Carson are spinning in their graves right now. Like as not they'd each blame the other for this.'' Ben Stone took a step back from the scene. He'd been the police chief of Mission Creek, the town that had slowly grown up and around the Lone Star Country Club that the once best friends had created, cutting the acreage equally out of both their properties before a blood feud had rent them apart, for more years than he was happy about. Agitated, he ran a hand through his salt-and-pepper hair. At 6'2'' he all but dwarfed the woman beside him.

Damn it all to hell, it wasn't supposed to have happened this way.

He shifted his keen eyes to her profile. If she lied, he'd know. Bonnie Brannigan was one of those scattered, flighty women who couldn't be secretive even if her life depended on it. ''You didn't see or hear anything, did you Bonnie?''

''No.'' Wiping away traces of the tear, she shook her head. ''I was in my office when this awful thing happened.'' Still dazed, she turned to look at him, fear in her clear-water blue eyes. ''You don't think this is like that terrible bombing in Oklahoma, do you?''

It astounded him how far off the mark she was. A tinge of relief wafted through the wall of frustration that surrounded him.

''That was a federal building, Bonnie, not a place where people like to come to talk over how much money they have.'' He watched firefighters scrambling out of the way as an outer wall fell. ''Maybe it was just an accident. Who knows?'' Playing out his role of the big protector, he slipped a comforting arm around her shoulders. It wasn't a hardship. Even though a grandmother, the curvaceous Bonnie Brannigan was still very much an attractive woman. And even better, right now she was no threat to him. "But we'll find out, by and by. Don't go troubling that pretty little head of yours."

Bonnie smiled, relieved to have someone in charge taking over. She loved her job at the club, but there were times, such as now, when she definitely felt in over her head. That was why she relied so heavily on people like Yance Ingram, the head of security at the club. She recalled that Ben had been the one to bring Yance to her attention.

Funny how thoughts just popped out of nowhere at a time like this.

"I suppose it could have been worse," she murmured, attempting to console herself. She looked at Stone, realizing that had to sound callous, given the circumstances. There were at least two known dead, perhaps more. "I mean, this could have happened during the busy part of the day."

Stone nodded, looking toward the body bags just being zipped closed by two of his men. The burned bodies had been pulled out of the wreckage that had been, until an hour ago, the main dining area of the Men's Grill.

"Just two fatalities." The wrong ones. A man and a woman. Their misfortune for being in the wrong place at the wrong time. "Do you know who they were?"

Were. The word had such a terrible ring to it. She nodded.

"Daniel and Meg Anderson." She'd stopped by

their table not fifteen minutes before the blast, asking if everything was to their liking. Admiring how much Jake had grown since the last time she'd seen him. Bonnie fought back a fresh wave of sorrow. "It's awful, just awful." Shivering again, she ran well-manicured hands along her arms to ward off a chill that no heat could chase away.

He had no idea what goaded him on. Instinct, probably. The security guards who had scrambled out of the burning building, soot all over their smart blue blazers and crisp gray slacks, had said that there appeared to be no one left within the area where the bomb and the accompanying fire had hit. There was no need to risk his life by diving back into the flames before they became entirely overwhelming to satisfy himself that everyone was out. His chief had ordered everyone clear of the building.

But one of the witnesses had mentioned something about thinking he had heard a child scream a heartbeat after the explosion. That had been enough to make Adam go back.

That and the memory of the child he hadn't been able to save from another inferno. His own child. And his wife.

The memory of that clung to him, riding the truck beside him with each fire he went to. No matter how many people Adam Collins had saved since that awful night two years ago when his small family had died in the flames within his house, it didn't ease his pain. He suspected it never would.

Taking deep breaths through his mask, Adam

forged farther into the burning building. The heat was all around him as broad, decorative beams above him groaned dangerously, threatening to snap in half at any moment.

He should be withdrawing.

He pushed on instead.

His captain's voice ordering him to turn back echoed in his head as he made his way through the blinding sheets of fire.

He almost missed him.

If he hadn't stumbled just then, trying to avoid falling debris, Adam wouldn't have seen him. The small, curled up form of a boy lying on the floor, covered with plaster.

At first he thought he was hallucinating. The boy looked so much like Bobby. But when he drew closer, fighting the flames for possession of a floor that was quickly eroding beneath his feet, Adam saw that it wasn't Bobby, wasn't a hallucination, it was a child. A small, unconscious little boy.

Scooping up the limp body, Adam fought his way back out.

Timber cracked and collapsed, nearly felling him. Blocking his path. With one arm wrapped around the boy, he picked another path, praying his luck would hold out one more time. Not for himself, but for the boy. Maybe that was why he'd been able to save so many people, because he didn't care if he lived or died. It allowed him that tiny extra edge that the other firefighters, with so much to live for, so much to lose, didn't have. It completely did away with any natural impulse to hesitate.

Light worked its way through the tunnel of smoke and flames. An exit.

Hang on, kid, we're almost there.

With a burst of adrenaline, Adam ran the rest of the way, making it out just in time. Behind him, the ceiling collapsed completely, making passage impossible. Had he hesitated for even a second, he and the boy would have been walled in.

"Oh my God, look!" Bonnie cried, pointing a crimson nail toward the far side of the blockaded area where the fire still raged. She covered her mouth with both hands as shock registered. In her devastation, she'd forgotten all about the boy. "He found him, he found Jake!"

Stone, talking to several of his men, his mind scrambling to put together the shard-like pieces of an explanation for what had transpired here this morning, looked up sharply at the sound of Bonnie's shrill, eager cry.

His eyes narrowed as he saw the firefighter miraculously emerge from the flames with the limp body of a boy pressed close to his chest.

His shoved his fisted hands deep into the pockets of his jacket.

"Looks like we got ourselves a hero," he announced to the general populace that was now milling around what was deemed the social center of Lone Star County as well as Mission Creek.

As cheers went up, Stone exchanged glances with Yance Ingram, the man who had once been his commanding officer in the Marines. A man after his own heart. He needed to talk to Ingram, to get the answers to questions he couldn't risk asking out loud in front of the crowd.

Ed Bancroft moved closer to him, a grim, wary look on his long, square face as he looked at his superior. "That's the boy," he confirmed. The boy he'd told Stone had looked into the security room.

Stone set his mouth hard. Damn it, he hated loose ends.

But as he came closer to the firemen, he saw that the boy's small chest wasn't moving. Maybe there was no need for concern after all.

Bonnie's stiletto heels sank into the damp ground with every step she took as she hurried over. "Is he all right?"

Adam didn't bother answering her. Instead, he ripped off his mask and helmet, his attention riveted on the boy he had rescued.

"I need help here!" he shouted without looking up.

The demand was issued to the paramedics who'd accompanied the fire trucks to the country club at the first sound of the alarm. But even before any of them managed to materialize at his elbow, Adam was employing CPR. One hand over the other, he pressed down hard on the boy's chest while counting to five in his mind.

The white patches of snow on the ground contrasted sharply with the dark, sooty layer of dirt along every part of the boy's blistered, burned body. Adam tried not to think about anything except getting the boy's chest to move, getting him to breathe on his own. The small chest felt so fragile. If he pressed too hard, he was afraid he might crush it.

He repeated the cycle twice, first pressing down on the boy's chest, then breathing into his mouth. Finally, the boy stirred, his lids fluttering, then opening. He looked directly into Adam's eyes.

Adam felt as if something had hit him smack in his chest with the force of an anvil.

"We can take over from here, buddy." K.C., one of the paramedics, firmly but gently nudged Adam aside. Gently, because they all knew that after two years the firefighter was no closer to being over the loss of his wife and son than he'd been the evening the tragedy had occurred.

Adam felt something take hold of his hand. When he looked down, he saw that the boy had wrapped his small, grimy, burned fingers around it. He knew that the very effort must have hurt terribly. The boy's grasp was not strong. It would have taken next to nothing to break the hold.

But the connection was far stronger than any steel wire could have ever managed. Adam couldn't pull his hand away. The boy's eyes wouldn't release him.

Adam heard the captain coming up behind him, felt a fatherly hand on his shoulder he neither related to nor resented.

"Anyone know who this boy is?" Captain MacIntire addressed his words to anyone in the immediate vicinity.

With careful steps, Bonnie moved closer to them. There were fresh tears shimmering in her eyes.

"That's Jake Anderson." She pressed her lips together, her heart going out to the boy. "Those were his parents you just...you just..." She couldn't make herself finish her statement.

She didn't have to.

Someone at the baseline of the fire called to MacIntire and he hurried away, all under the watchful eye of Chief Stone.

Adam made up his mind. "I'm going with the boy."

Working over Jake, K.C. slanted a look toward Adam. There was understanding in the paramedic's eyes. But sympathy, they'd learned, was the last thing anyone offered Adam Collins.

"Suit yourself." K.C. snapped the legs on the gurney and they popped upright. With Adam walking alongside him, holding the boy's hand, he guided the gurney to the rear of the ambulance. "But being the good Samaritan won't keep the captain from getting on your case for playing Superman again."

"Yeah, but it'll postpone it for a while." Adam stepped back to allow the gurney to be hoisted into the ambulance. Jake's fingers remained around his. Adam twisted around to maintain the connection, then got into the ambulance himself.

Dr. Tracy Walker felt beat and ready to call it a day. And it wasn't even one o'clock.

She felt as if she'd been running on fast-forward all morning, with no signs of a letup anytime soon. It had started when her alarm had failed to go off at five. Five a.m. was not her idea of an ideal hour to get up, but it would have given her sufficient time to pull herself together for the surgery she had to perform this morning. Five o'clock came and went, as did six and then almost seven.

Fortunately, Tracy had what she fondly liked to refer to as an alarm pig, a gentle, quick-footed Vietnamese potbellied pig that was still very much a baby and went by the name of Petunia. Petunia, it turned out, was trainable and far more intelligent than some of the people Tracy knew.

At five to seven, Petunia had snuggled in at her feet and tickled her awake. Any one-sided dialogue Tracy had felt up to rendering was immediately curtailed the instant she'd rolled over in her bed and saw that according to her non-ringing clock, she had exactly twenty minutes to shower, eat and get herself to the hospital for the skin grafting surgery she was scheduled to perform.

Weighing her options and the somewhat seductive power hot water had over her, Tracy decided to sacrifice the shower and breakfast as she hurried into clothes, put out a bowl of fresh water for Petunia and threw herself behind the wheel of her car in less time than it took for an ordinary citizen to floss their teeth.

As she ran out the door she promised a disgruntled Petunia to return during her own lunch break to feed her choice leftovers from the refrigerator. Petunia had said nothing.

With one eye on the rearview mirror, watching for dancing blue and red lights, Tracy had bent a few speeding rules and made it to the operating room with two minutes to spare.

The three-hour surgery had been as successful as

possible, given the circumstances. There were no instant cures, no huge miracles in her line of work. Only many small miracles that were eventually hooked up into one large one. She was a pediatric burn specialist, and there was nothing in the world she would rather have been, even though it meant having her heart torn out of her chest whenever she saw another victim being wheeled into the hospital. Pain went with the territory. But someone had to help these children and she had elected herself to be one of the ones on the front lines. It gave her life a purpose.

"Out of my way, Myra," she wearily told a nurse who had somehow materialized in her path. "I'm on my way home to feed a hungry pig."

But the dark-skinned woman shook her head. "'Fraid your boyfriend's going to have to wait, Doctor," the thrice-divorced woman told her. "We just got a call in on the scanner. There's been a bombing at the Lone Star Country Club."

"A bombing?" Here? In Mission Creek? They were a peaceful little town of some twenty thousand people. Who would want to bomb them? Had the world gone completely crazy? "Does anyone know who did it?"

"Beats me," Myra lamented. "But dispatch says they're bringing in a little boy who's going to need your gentle touch."

Tracy took the new sterile, yellow paper gown Myra held up for her and donned it to cover her regular scrubs. "Do we know how many people were hurt?"

"About fifteen or so." The wail of approaching

sirens disturbed the tranquil atmosphere, growing louder by the second. ''But according to the dispatch, there were only two fatalities.'' Myra's dark eyes met hers. ''The kid's parents.''

''Oh God,'' Tracy groaned just as the emergency room doors parted and the ambulances began arriving.

First on the scene were the two paramedics with the boy Tracy assumed was her patient. Hurrying alongside of the gurney, holding tightly onto the boy's hand, was a firefighter, still wearing his heavy yellow slicker. The sight had a dramatic impact.

A relative? she wondered.

The next moment, Tracy was looking at the boy and ceased wondering about anything else.

Chapter 2

She never got used to it.

Never got used to seeing the anguish in their eyes, on their faces, could never anesthetize herself not to take note of the pitiful, fearful conditions in which so many of her patients arrived.

Tracy never bothered wasting time trying to find answers to unanswered questions or an order to the universe. She was just grateful that her training allowed her to make a difference in these children's lives, however small. To help start these innocent victims, who had unwittingly stood in the path of a cruel and feelingless fate, back on the road to recovery.

She gave each patient a hundred and ten percent of her skills and, despite numerous warnings to the contrary by superiors and friends who cared about her, a piece of her heart.

It was no different with this newest victim that the

two paramedics brought her. The instant she saw the terrified look on the boy's face, she forgot about the firefighter hurrying at his side.

Petunia and her dilemma were placed on temporary hold in her mind as well. Tracy tried not to think of what the small pig might begin eating in lieu of her belated breakfast. That was something she would have to deal with later.

Listening to the paramedics rattle off vital signs, Tracy shot questions back at them and swiftly assessed the boy's injuries. She did her best not to disturb the raw, blistered flesh on his arms and legs.

"Put him in trauma room three," she instructed the orderly who'd rushed up to the first gurney with her. "I need someone to cut off his clothes. And be gentle about it," she added. Looking down at the sooty, bruised face, she did her best to make her smile encouraging. "You're going to be fine, honey, I promise. Can you tell me your name?"

The only response she got was a whimper.

There was something about the way he seemed to stare right through her that chilled her heart.

Shock, she thought. She felt tears forming at the corners of her eyes. Moving quickly, Tracy helped guide the gurney into the trauma room.

"That's okay, sweetheart. I don't need your name right now. Mine's Dr. Walker in case you need to call me later." Belatedly, she realized that the firefighter was still with them and about to enter the trauma room. She shook her head, automatically placing a hand against his chest. It felt as if she was pressing against a wall, not a man. "I'm sorry, you're going to have to stay out here."

"I won't get in the way." Adam had no idea why, but he wanted to be in there with the boy, to somehow assure him, as well as himself, that everything was going to be all right.

"I'm sorry, only staff members are allowed past these doors." He looked perturbed at the restriction. She paused longer than she should have. "Are you a relative?"

He shook his head. "No. I just wanted to make sure he was all right."

She of all people understood becoming involved with the people you were responsible for saving. She offered him an encouraging smile. "I'll let you know as soon as I can. Why don't you wait in the hall?" She made the suggestion just before she slipped behind the door.

Tracy quickly crossed to the examining table. Her team had transferred the boy while she'd hung back with the firefighter. The orderly, Max, pushed the gurney out of the way.

With a nod of her head, she was all business again. "Okay, people, every moment we waste is another moment he has to suffer."

She worked as swiftly as she dared, making the little boy as comfortable as possible under the circumstances, issuing orders to the two nurses who buffered her sides. They moved like a well-oiled machine. A machine whose only purpose was to help this small child who had been in the wrong place at the wrong time.

Tracy checked her tears until after the job was over. Unleashing them wouldn't do the boy any good.

What the hell was taking so long?

And what was he doing here, anyway? Adam wondered, exasperated with himself. This wasn't part of his job. His job had ended the instant he had brought the boy out of the burning building.

He paced the length of the hallway, his impatience mounting with each step he took. That was his job description, saving people from burning buildings, and he'd done that. End of story.

So why was he here, pacing up and down a pastel-colored hallway, sweaty, sooty and smelling of smoke when he should be at the fire station, taking a well-earned shower and trying to wind down from a job well done?

He had no reasonable explanation, even for himself. All he knew was that the frightened look he'd seen in the boy's wide blue eyes when they had stared up into his had transcended any logic Adam could offer either to himself or to his superior when the time came.

It wasn't like him to get all wound up like this about someone he'd pulled to safety.

And yet, here he was, wound up tighter than a timpani drum.

The door opened and Adam snapped to attention, his body rigid. He was at the doctor's side, his six-three frame looming over her five-foot five-inch one before the door had a chance to swing closed.

Adam didn't attempt to second-guess the expression on her face. "How is he?" he demanded.

His tone had taken him out of the realm in which her assumption had placed him: that of rescuer and rescuee. For the firefighter to look so concerned, when rescuing people out of burning buildings was, if not a daily, then at least an occupational occurrence, there had to be something more going on.

Maybe they actually were related somehow and for his own reasons he just didn't want to admit it. Even given the boy's age, there seemed to be no other explanation for why one of the county's firefighters would have accompanied someone he'd rescued and then hung around the hallway, waiting to hear about his condition.

She was too tired to make an educated guess and almost too tired to ask.

Tracy pulled off her mask, letting it hang from its strings about her neck. "He's still in shock. Pretty harrowing experience for a kid to go through. But his wounds aren't quite as extensive or serious as they first appeared. I was afraid some of them were third-degree, but most of them are second-degree and some are even first." She knew she didn't have to explain the difference or the significance to this man. "But any number you assign to them, they hurt like hell." Summoning her energy, she framed a question for him. "Is it true?"

With everything that happened, he couldn't help wondering if he'd done the boy a favor, saving him. The kid was in pain, about to undergo surgical procedures that were undoubtedly excruciating and the bomb had made him an orphan on top of that. It was a huge load for someone so small.

He frowned. Adam had no idea what the doctor was talking about. "Is what true?"

She had to concentrate not to wrap her arms around herself in a bid for comfort. Although she'd never been close to her, she'd lost her mother when she was twenty-two. It had hurt then. How much worse did it feel to be so young when that happened? And to be completely orphaned on top of that?

Did the boy even know his parents were dead?

Maybe she'd misheard. A glimmer of hope flashed for a moment. "You said his parents were killed in the blast?"

The firefighter's chiseled chin hardened even more. "Yeah."

She'd navigated life's rougher seas by clinging to optimism. "Then I guess he was lucky."

While he'd waited, Adam'd had time to call back to the station house to tell them that he'd be at County General for awhile. McGuire had told him that according to the manager of the club, the boy had gone off to the men's room minutes before the blast. The woman had volunteered that he was an only child. That left him alone.

"Depends on your definition of luck."

What a strange, somber man, Tracy thought. She wondered if there was someone in his life, or if being alone had made him so bitter sounding.

"I'd say being alive is lucky." She glanced back toward the trauma room. She'd given the boy a sedative to help him rest. "Being alive is always better than the alternative."

Adam thought of his own life, a life that had been empty and bleak these past two years despite all the efforts of his siblings and extended family to bring him around. "I suppose that really depends on your point of view."

Turning toward him, Tracy studied his face thoughtfully. He was younger than he sounded, she realized. But his eyes were old. And angry. "Rather a fatalistic attitude for a firefighter."

He shrugged carelessly. "It's what sees me through the day."

Tracy prided herself on being a decent judge of people. She'd sized him up and decided that this man wasn't quite as emotionless as he would have liked to believe himself to be. If he were, he wouldn't be standing here now, waiting to hear how the boy was.

Playing devil's advocate, she asked, "Then what are you doing here?"

His expression became unreadable. "Seeing about the boy."

She wanted him to say why. "You saved him."

He wouldn't have put it that way. "I pulled him out of the fire."

Tracy was far too tired to butt heads. "That you did, Mr.—?"

"Collins. Adam," he added after a beat.

Adam was surprised when she put out her hand to him and then took his when he made no move to do the same. "Tracy Walker. You wouldn't happen to know his name, would you?"

He'd overheard the blonde with the listing beehive hairdo, Bonnie something he recalled, say the boy's name when she was talking to the chief.

"Jake Anderson, I think."

Tracy nodded, taking in the information. "Well, no matter how you choose to put it, Collins, Jake owes his life to you."

The boy didn't owe him anything. It was he who owed the boy something for pulling him out of the jaws of death only to fling him back into a life that was filled with pain.

He nodded toward the trauma room. "What'll happen to him?"

Tracy assumed the firefighter was asking about treatment.

"Fortunately, we're prepared for his kind of case here at County General. A lot of hospitals aren't. We'll see to his wounds, help him heal." *At least physically,* she thought. "I might be wrong, but I don't think any skin grafts'll be necessary, so that's good."

She didn't look as if she should be dealing with things like burnt flesh and peeling skin. He could more readily see her indulging in a game of tennis or riding horses at the club, rather than leaning over an operating table trying to graft skin over a charred body. "And then?"

She didn't quite understand. "Then?"

He was thinking about the orphan part. Where did Jake go after he was released? "After you do your job and he's well, what happens to him then?"

She paused for a second to think. "Social services, I guess, until we can locate a relative."

Adam had a bad feeling about this. "And if there's no relative?"

"He goes into the system." Tracy crossed her arms in front of her, trying to get a handle on what was going on in Collins's head. "Are you usually this concerned about people you save from burning buildings?"

Adam had never cared for being questioned or analyzed. And he'd seen the woman's tears just before she'd withdrawn into the trauma room. "Do you usually cry over your patients?"

Tracy saw no shame in empathizing with her patients. The way she saw it, it made her human.

"All the time, Mr. Collins, all the time. When I can help them, when I can't. And when I hear about a little boy who has lost the two most precious people in his life at such a young age." She leveled her gaze at him. "What's your excuse?"

The woman's very body language challenged him. Scooping up the heavy yellow jacket from the chair where he'd left it, Adam punched his arms through the sleeves and pulled it closed. "I've got to be going."

Rather than let him go, Tracy hurried after him. The man had done something sensitive, it hadn't been her intent to chase him away.

"Wait." Adam stopped and turned around. Free of her surgical cap, her dark curly hair swirled around her face as she caught up to him. "I'm sorry. I didn't mean to sound as if I was being combative. It's just been one of those very long mornings, that's all. You were being a good guy, even if you weren't being very communicative, and I was being—'' Tracy paused and then smiled as she concluded, "Me, I guess. They tell me I talk before I think. Sometimes, they're right.''

His eyes narrowed. "They?''

"My friends.'' Her mouth softened as an almost pixieish smile graced her face. "You did good today, Adam Collins.'' And then, because something told her that the words were more applicable to him than to the child she had just worked over, she added, "And no matter how black the situation looks, it'll get better.''

How could she say something like that? How could she believe it? Doing what she did, day in, day out, seeing what she saw, how could she possibly pretend to believe what she'd just said?

The look he gave her made Tracy feel as if she were being X-rayed.

"You're sure about that?''

She was a firm believer in meeting darkness with sunshine. "As sure as I am that God made little green apples.''

His expression was incredulous. "What the hell is that supposed to mean?''

"I really don't know, but I heard it somewhere and I thought it sounded nice.'' She glanced at her watch. Trained pig or not, Petunia was going to start nibbling on the furniture legs any second now, if she hadn't already. She was a good little animal, as obedient as they came, but she was a pig and pigs ate anything when they were very, very hungry. Tracy knew she'd more than exceeded her grace period with Petunia. "Now if you'll excuse me, I have a pig to feed."

The woman was beginning to sound positively weird. "Is that some kind of an encrypted message?"

She cocked her head, as if to review her words and think. "Not that I'm aware of."

"You have a farm?" That would be the logical explanation. The hospital was in the heart of town, but maybe she lived beyond the city limits and was going home.

"No." Her grin widened. "I have a pig. A very sweet little Vietnamese potbellied pig who's as smart as a whip and right now, as hungry as a bear. I didn't have time to feed her this morning and if I don't get back to her soon, I might not have anything left in the apartment when I get home." About to dash off, Tracy stopped abruptly as a thought occurred to her. "Do you need a lift?"

Coming out of nowhere, her question caught him off guard. "What?"

"You came in with the boy in an ambulance," she recalled. "I don't figure the paramedics hung around waiting for you all this time. Do you want a lift to your fire station?"

He did, but he'd already decided to call a cab. Her offer, tendered so guilelessly, left him momentarily speechless. It just wasn't rational. "You don't even know me. Do you always give rides to strange men you don't know?"

She supposed if she had a choice, she would rather be too trusting than not trusting at all. "We both saved the same boy—in our own way," she allowed. Her eyes smiled at him. They were hazel, with sunshine in them. "I know you."

He had no idea how to respond to that. With a shrug, Adam fell into step beside her.

"How the hell did that bomb go off before they got inside?" Stone demanded of the short, squat head of security for the Lone Star Country Club. He towered over the older man who had once sent fear into his own heart. But that was back when he was a wet-behind-the-ears marine recruit. The tables had now turned. Now Yance Ingram reported to him. And the report wasn't good. "I thought you said you knew what you were doing."

Yance tugged on the ends of his graying mustache, working to contain his anger. He wasn't accustomed to being spoken to this way. "Don't take that tone with me, boy. I wasn't the one who screwed up."

Huffing his displeasure like a runaway locomotive, Stone circled around the offending man, one of his handpicked, chosen inner circle.

Served him right for not seeing to it himself, Stone thought. But he'd deliberately left the details up to a select few, wanting to distance himself from the actual deed as much as possible. Blame had a way of smearing once it was voiced, and at all costs, he was trying to protect the sweet deal that had all but fallen into his lap at a time when he most needed it.

Wouldn't have needed anything if Susanne hadn't turned out to be a first-class bitch, he thought darkly.

It hadn't been enough for her to up-end his life by

divorcing him and taking away his daughters, she had to demand a pound of flesh from him as well. A monthly pound of flesh in the form of staggering alimony payments. It was like paying for a meal long after the dishes were cleared away. The alimony payments, on top of the child support he was doling out plus the alimony he was still paying to his first wife, had turned him into a man with his back pressed against a wall full of sharp, rusty nails. He was desperate.

That was how El Jefe had found him, desperate. The self-proclaimed new kingpin of the Central American drug trade had a nose for desperate men who could be useful to him. The partnership they had struck up proved to be a lucrative one for both of them. Drug money came into the States, to be carefully banked and deposited via money orders into a bank account he'd personally set up for El Jefe's legitimate holding company, Emeralda. The money went back to El Jefe for business transactions, minus a healthy cut for his part in the laundering.

It enabled Stone to pay his debts, his monthly penance—alimony, he thought cynically, the wound that keeps on giving—and still have a nice piece of change to squirrel away at the end of each month until the day he could convince Joan Cooper to marry him.

That was all he wanted, a fresh start with a good, decent woman and enough money to buy and sell this godforsaken little hellhole he found himself in charge of.

But the operation required more than just his being involved. By its very nature, it required that he take men into his confidence to use as his soldiers. So he found them. Men he trusted as much as he was willing to trust anyone. They'd formed what he laughingly referred to as The Lion's Den, taking the name from the pin the mayor had been awarding people within town for services rendered beyond the call of duty for the past ten years or so. Stone had taken to giving a pin of his own to the men he entrusted to serve him. The only difference being that the lion in his pin had three legs rather than four. The way the pin was fashioned, the difference wasn't noticeable unless you were looking for it.

That was how they all knew one another within this secret society of theirs. But Stone wasn't some blind optimist, willing just to let things see to themselves of their own accord. He watched the men who held not only their fate but inadvertently his in their hands. Watched them like a hawk. Ordinarily. But this one time, he'd rested a little too easy, relying on Yance's extensive expertise with explosives. There was supposed to be none better.

All it had gotten him was two dead citizens and one possible live witness. None of whom had been his original target.

Stone lowered his voice to keep it from carrying out of the office. "Then who did screw up?" he demanded. "You were the one with the dynamite, you were the one who planted it in the display right by the table that'd been reserved—"

Ingram's small eyes narrowed into slits. "I set it for five minutes after the hour the reservation was made for. As agreed."

"You should have set it for ten minutes after the hour," Stone retorted.

"Then we should have agreed to ten," Ingram countered.

The argument was going nowhere. And even if it were resolved, it wouldn't change anything, Stone thought darkly. He was supposed to be resting easy at this point, not find himself in the middle of a mess. Now everyone was waiting for him to head up a task force to investigate the bombing.

Rumors were already flying right and left as to its origin. Some, like that bubbleheaded Brannigan woman, thought it might be the work of terrorists, while others thought it might even be a disgruntled club member, taking out his frustration. Still others thought it was the work of the Texas mob. Nobody even came close to the real reason and he meant to make sure it remained that way.

The short fuse that comprised his temper insisted on lighting anyway. "Damn it, Ingram, it was your job to make sure this kind of thing didn't happen."

His nerves taut, Ingram's face turned almost beet-red as he snapped, "I'm not God, boy."

Stone ran a narrow, almost artistic-looking hand through his hair, cursing roundly. The opportunity had passed. His target had left the grounds shaken, but unscathed. Which meant that everything he'd worked so hard to build up might be in jeopardy.

If his connection to El Jefe ever came to light…

Shaking his head, he forced the thought aside. Right now, he had a more immediate problem to deal with right here in his own backyard.

The apology to Ingram nearly choked him, but he needed the man, now more than ever.

With effort, he forced it out, then turned his attention to damage control.

Pulling up in the driveway, right in front of the fire truck that the men had just finished cleaning after the ordeal at the country club, Tracy cheerfully announced to Adam, "This is your stop."

She'd gone more than a little out of her way to drop the firefighter at his station, but she didn't mind. The drive over from the hospital would have been a silent one had she not kept up a steady stream of conversation. For all intents and purposes, it was more of a monologue than a conversation, garnering little more than grunts and one-word answers from the noble firefighter sitting in the passenger seat of her '95 Mustang convertible.

"And I can't say I'm not relieved," she told him. When he looked at her quizzically, Tracy added with a bright smile, "You damn near talked my ear off."

The absurd comment coaxed what passed for a smile from Adam's lips. After all, she had done him a favor, even if he hadn't asked her to. "I'm not usually very talkative."

She widened her eyes in feigned surprise. "You're kidding."

He snorted, getting out of the car. "Didn't seem to bother you any, I noticed. You talk enough for three people."

Not three, she thought, but maybe two. "I don't much care for silence," she admitted.

He preferred silence himself. ''You should try it sometime,'' he told her pointedly.

Tracy took no offense. ''Deal. If you try talking sometime.'' Not about to leave herself open for a smart rejoinder, she shifted gears and began backing out of the driveway. ''See you around, Collins,'' she called out.

Vince McGuire, a firefighter who had joined the staff at the fire station shortly after Adam had arrived, approached him, an appreciative look on his face as he watched Tracy pull away.

''We'd wondered where you'd gotten to.'' He nodded at the departing vehicle and its driver. ''Bring back a souvenir from the fire?''

Turning on his heel, Adam began walking into the fire station. He didn't even bother looking at the other man. ''Stick it in your ear, McGuire.''

''That wasn't exactly where I had in mind,'' McGuire said with a laugh as he hurried to catch up.

Chapter 3

Adam sighed in frustration as he let the receiver drop into the cradle. It was raining outside the window of his first-floor apartment, one of those dark and gloomy January days that made people long for spring and feel it was never going to arrive.

The mood within his apartment was just as dark and gloomy.

He couldn't get Jake Anderson off his mind.

The boy was about the same age as his own son had been when he'd lost him. At first glance, Jake had even looked like Bobby, the same silky blond hair, the same slight, delicate build. And the eyes, there was just something about the look in Jake's blue eyes that had worked its way under his skin, refusing to leave him alone.

Walking out of the living room, Adam crossed to the kitchen more on automatic pilot than by conscious thought. Ordinarily, he made a point to shed the events of the day along with his uniform when he left the station house. It was the only way he'd found he could survive.

But not this time.

This time, he could see Jake's face, could see his burned and bruised little body, could even smell the smoke that had surrounded the boy like a malevolent envelope every time his mind began to stray.

In an attempt to free himself and put the whole incident behind him, Adam decided to see what he could find out about Jake having any next of kin who would take him in.

A cursory effort had yielded nothing. Getting off duty, he'd stopped by the country club and asked a still very much shaken Bonnie Brannigan if she could give him the Andersons' address, since it had to be on file in the membership listing. Once he had the address, he'd gone to the Andersons' neighborhood and knocked on the doors of several of their neighbors. No one knew anything. The Andersons had been gregarious people, but neither had ever mentioned any extended family. A woman who lived across the street from them had told him that Meg had once mentioned that she and her husband were both only children. And apparently nobody had ever seen any grandparents pulling up into the Andersons' driveway to pay a visit during any of the holidays.

Facing a dead end, he'd dug a little deeper.

Adam had just gotten off the telephone with a friend of his whose sister worked in the social services department that would have jurisdiction over

Mission Creek. He hated calling in favors, but for reasons he didn't want to examine, this had become important to him.

He encountered the same dead end he'd found by going to the Andersons' neighborhood. There was no next of kin. No doting grandparent, no busy long-lost uncle or vivacious aunt to come to Jake's aid and take him in.

According to Rick Foster's sister, Jenny, the preliminary investigation indicated that the Andersons seemed to have no family whatsoever except for some distant second cousin.

Adam had no reason to doubt Jenny Foster's findings. She'd been at her job over ten years and knew the system inside and out.

The system.

That's the way that lady doctor had referred to it. The system. He didn't want the boy to be eaten up by the system, with no one to care for him, no one to make the night terrors go away, the way he had for Bobby when his son had woken up in the middle of the night, screaming and shaking.

Adam sat down at his small kitchen table, picking up the roast beef sandwich he'd haphazardly thrown together for lunch just before his phone had rung. He bit into it, his mind reviewing the meager facts. The only relative Jenny had come up with was a distant cousin on Meg Anderson's side. A forty-three-year-old twice-divorced anthropologist who was currently on a dig somewhere in Africa, nobody knew exactly where.

Maybe he could be persuaded to take the boy, but

Adam doubted it. It was a long shot at best and besides, Jake needed someone now. Mayonnaise
leeched out of Adam's sandwich on one side, taking
a piece of lettuce with it. It fell on his paper plate
with a glop, but he didn't notice. He was too busy
thinking.

He didn't like the idea of the boy facing all this
alone.

This was Adam's downtime. Like any firefighter,
he worked two days on, two days off. What he normally did during this time was unwind, put his professional life as far out of his mind as possible. But
Jake's eyes wouldn't let him. Try though he might,
Adam couldn't seem to separate his thoughts,
couldn't shove them into the neat little cubicles where
he always pushed them in. Despite his best efforts, it
had happened.

His professional life had seeped into his private
life.

There was no denying it. The boy he had rescued
from the Lone Star Country Club fire had gotten to
him.

He needed to do something to work this out of his
system. With no set plan for the day, Adam decided
it might be a good idea to pay a visit to the hospital
to see how Jake was coming along.

Maybe if the boy was mending well, he could stop
thinking about him so much.

Stone paced around his office. He was beyond angry. It had been a simple, simple plan. Nothing was
supposed to have gone wrong. And yet, everything

had. And it threatened to continue to go wrong, bringing down everything around him. It was like when you pull an apple out of the bottom row of neatly arranged fruit—an avalanche resulted.

He couldn't have that. Wouldn't have that.

Swinging around, he looked at the man who was the latest recipient of his foul mood. Ed Bancroft. The man responsible for leaving the security room door ajar while they were transferring the sacks of money. The sacks were normally retained in the back closet of the security room after the money arrived from Central America, but before the purchase of non-traceable money orders.

Simple. Yet in jeopardy now.

He'd had his doubts about bringing Bancroft on. The man was weak enough to be malleable, but he had the one thing that had made many a scheme run afoul: the remnants of a conscience.

He just had to see to it that he kept Bancroft too intimidated to even think of allowing that conscience to dictate any of his actions.

"I want to know what that kid saw, understand?"

Bancroft had been the one to look up and see the boy peeking into the security office just as the green canvas bags were being loaded onto the truck.

"The bags were closed, Chief. There's no way anyone could have known what was in them. Besides, I saw the kid before the ambulance took him away. He was in pretty bad shape. He might not make it. And even if he does, I'm not sure if I'll be able to see him."

It was the wrong thing to say. Anything beyond

"Yes, Chief" would have been. Stone's eyes reduced to small, malevolent slits.

"What are you, a complete cretin? We're talking about some six-year-old kid—"

"Five," Bancroft corrected automatically, then instantly regretted it. The chief didn't like being corrected.

"Five," Stone spat out. "You've got a badge. That gives you access to anybody. We're supposed to be investigating the bombing, remember? I'm heading up the task force." Which was the ultimate joke, seeing as how he'd been the one to set the wheels in motion. But that was what made his position so sweet. Since he had control over everything that went on in and around Mission Creek, he could squash anyone who might interfere with his operation.

Like he should have been able to squash that damned aging commando, he thought darkly.

Gathering his thoughts together, he tried to remember which of the men in the Lion's Den were currently available. He didn't trust Bancroft going out alone.

"I want you to take Malloy with you and go question the kid." He nailed the tall, narrow-chested man with a look. "And don't scare him, just get him to tell you exactly what he saw. Maybe things aren't as black as they seem." But Stone doubted it. He'd been born a pessimist and hadn't been disappointed yet. "And next time, make sure the goddamn inner door is closed before you start moving the bags out."

Bancroft made a fruitless attempt to absolve himself. "It wasn't my fault, Chief. I wasn't anywhere near it and I wasn't the last man in—"

"Doesn't matter whose fault it was." Other than the fact that he was going to make the miserable bastard pay, whoever it was, Stone thought. Taking a step, he got directly into the other policeman's face. "Know this. If one of us goes down, we all could go down. Do I make myself clear?"

Like a newly recruited marine trying not to buckle before his drill sergeant in boot camp, Bancroft squared his thin shoulders. "Yes, sir."

"Good, now get going." Stone pushed the other man toward the door. "The sooner I know where we stand, the better."

In the doorway, struck by a bolt of either duty or momentary insanity, Bancroft hesitated, then said, "Chief, Westin's gone."

The dark look Stone gave him told Bancroft the chief was already aware of this salient piece of information. Bancroft quickly darted out the door before the second wave of fallout began.

The boy had been on Tracy's mind all night. She didn't think of him as another burn victim, or even think of him by his name. She thought of Jake as the boy with the sad eyes.

She didn't think she'd ever seen eyes that sad before.

All things considered, it was a routine enough procedure for her. She'd sedated Jake yesterday before treating his wounds. He'd been bathed in cool water and moist bandages had been applied to the burned skin. Pumped full of antibiotics to prevent any infections from setting in, there was every reason in the world to believe Jake Anderson would make a full and complete recovery, given time.

Still, she'd sat by his bed after she'd returned from feeding Petunia, waiting for Jake to wake up. She didn't want to have him open his eyes to an empty room. When he'd finally woken up, hours later, she'd gently talked to him, but there had been no response. He'd just lain there, staring at the ceiling.

At first, she'd thought he was disoriented, or frightened, but after a while she realized that he had gone off somewhere, into his own little world. A world where no one and nothing could enter. That included emotional pain. As gently as she could, though it hadn't been easy for her, she'd told him about his parents. There'd been no response, no reaction.

She was certain that on some level, Jake already knew his parents were dead. He hadn't cried out for them, hadn't made a sound at all. As long as he stayed within the confines of the silence he'd created, he didn't have to admit that he was alone.

Concerned, she'd called down Lydia Sanchez, the head of the child psychology department at the hospital, for a consultation.

Lydia had spent a half hour with the boy, reviewing his files and talking to him. There had been no response for her, either.

"It's self-preservation," Lydia had told her outside the boy's room. "His mind can't deal with the tragedy, can't deal with the words, so for him all words are dead. He's mute."

"Is he traumatically deaf, too?" Tracy knew there was no physical reason for it. She'd had several tests performed that showed there was no trauma to his brain, no injuries to his auditory nerves and none to his throat or vocal chords.

"No," Lydia had told her, looking at Jake through the glass that separated the boy from them. "He can hear you. Whether he's processing the words is another matter. I think he is, but—" she shrugged, uncertain whether she was right or not.

"How long will he stay this way?" Tracy had wanted to know.

"Hard to tell. He might start talking again by this evening. Then again, this might go on for some time."

"Months?" Tracy guessed.

"Possibly. But doubtful," Lydia had said in the next breath. "He's young. They heal faster when they're young."

At least she could hope, Tracy thought.

She looked at Jake now, newly changed bandages covering parts of his arms and legs, as well as his torso. His face, because it had been buried beneath his arm, had mercifully been spared. He lay on his back on the egg-crate mattress meant to alleviate some of his discomfort by redistributing his weight. Staring at the ceiling, he seemed completely oblivious to the fact that she was there. She talked anyway, keeping her voice as bright and cheery as possible.

"We're going to let you slide for a little while, Jake. But tomorrow, we're going to get you up and moving. Don't want those limbs of yours to get soft now, do we?'' She looked at him, but there was no indication on his face that he even heard a single word. ''You have to exercise your muscles, you know. Use them or lose them. We've got a neat physical therapist. Her name's Randi. Kind of a funny name for a girl, huh?''

There was no response, only the soft sounds of the monitors that surrounded him, keeping tabs on his vital signs.

Tracy pushed on. ''But she's very nice. She's got a little boy a bit younger than you are, so she knows all about—''

She stopped as the door abruptly opened and two uniformed policemen, grim-faced and very official looking, entered the room.

Tracy's voice changed to one of authority. ''May I help you, Officers?''

Kyle Malloy took the lead. Shorter, stockier, he had no patience with excuses or anything that got in his way. His eyes washed over her quickly, missing nothing and lingering on the soft silhouette evident within the opened lab coat that draped the woman.

''We're Officers Malloy and Bancroft.'' He gestured vaguely to indicate who was who. ''We'd like to ask the boy a few questions about what happened at the Lone Star Country Club yesterday.''

She was surprised to see Jake's eyes shift toward the men, his gaze intent. He wasn't as unaware of things as he was trying to pretend. It was a hopeful sign, Tracy thought.

She moved protectively to the foot of Jake's bed,

blocking the policeman's direct access to him. "I'm afraid that's not possible."

Bancroft began to say something, but Malloy cut him off. His smile disappeared. "And just who are you?"

"Dr. Tracy Walker." She saw his eyes go to the ID tag she and the rest of the staff wore on a navy blue string around their necks. She didn't care for the time delay before he raised them again to her face. "I'm his doctor—"

The smug smile returned to his lips. "We won't be too long," Malloy promised her. "But the chief wants us to talk to everyone who was anywhere in the area, and from preliminary indications by the crime scene investigators, this boy had a ringside table with his mama and papa. Can't have a bomber running around, now can we?"

Tracy resented the slight condescending tone she heard in the policeman's voice. A lot of people had trouble taking her seriously. She knew that part of it was because, even at thirty, she looked younger than her age. That had always gotten in her way.

But part of the reason for the tone, she surmised, was because of some male superiority thing that was going on inside of Officer Malloy's head.

Either way, she wasn't about to allow them to badger Jake.

"No," she smiled tightly, momentarily playing along with the role she'd been assigned, "we can't. But Jake still can't tell you anything."

"That's for us to decide, little lady," Malloy informed her. "You never know when the slightest clue might just break open a case."

Tired of the game, Tracy dropped her tone. It was time to get these policemen to leave. Though he hadn't given any outward indication, something told Tracy that their presence here was agitating Jake. If nothing else, she wasn't about to have them continue talking about the bombing. He was upset enough as it was.

"Please, Officer, I've seen *Columbo*. Spare me the hype. Jake can't tell you anything because Jake can't talk."

Malloy exchanged glances with Bancroft. This was news to them.

After a beat, Malloy decided he wasn't buying it. The woman was stonewalling him. He wasn't about to return to the chief to tell him that he'd failed. It was a hell of a lot easier taking on this woman.

"What do you mean he can't talk? No one said anything about the boy being deaf and dumb."

Now she knew the man was an idiot. Tracy's anger took in his all but silent partner as she looked at both of them.

"The correct term," she informed Malloy tersely, "is hearing-and-speech impaired, and Jake Anderson wasn't—until the accident." She looked back at the still, bandaged body in the bed, giving Jake a reassuring smile he didn't seem to notice or acknowledge. She looked back at the two policemen. "He can hear you, but he doesn't speak."

"There's nothing wrong with him, is there?" Bancroft asked hesitantly. He fumbled when Tracy looked at him strangely. "I mean, there's no chance that he had any brain damage or anything, right?"

She couldn't read the other man's tone. Was that concern or disappointment she heard? Or something else?

"None that any of the tests have revealed. But he's been through a great deal of trauma caused by the bombing and the fire. He's sustained burns to over thirty percent of his body, not to mention the fact that he's suffered personal loss." She looked from one man to the other, assuming that the two policemen were both sensitive enough to understand the reason for the euphemism she was employing.

Malloy frowned, negating all thoughts of even cursory sensitivity being in the man's arsenal. "Right, it's too bad, still, we've got this investigation and we need to know what he saw, if anything."

Moving past Tracy, Bancroft approached the boy. "Did you see anyone maybe running from the scene, or anything unusual at all?"

"Maybe the two of you should be checked out for hearing problems," Tracy suggested angrily, getting in between Bancroft and the bed. "I just told you, Jake Anderson can't talk. He hasn't uttered a single word since they brought him in yesterday."

Malloy smirked at her, as if he thought that she was being simpleminded. "Maybe he's just playing a game, honey."

Tracy instantly felt her back going up. As far as she was concerned, she had put up with as much as she intended to.

"My name is not 'honey' and even if it were, you

don't have a right to call me by my first name unless I tell you you do.'' Her eyes darkened dangerously. Having to fight her way up to her position had taught her how to stand up to narrow-minded bigots. "Now I'd like to ask you to please leave—''

Afraid of arousing suspicion and creating waves that might draw too much attention, Bancroft tapped Malloy's shoulder. "Maybe we'd better.'' He began to leave, but Malloy dug in.

The policeman took a step around the bed toward her. "Look, honey, this is official business. So whether you like it or not—''

"You heard the lady, officers. The boy can't help you.'' Adam strode into the room, his eyes as dark as the day was outside. The package he'd brought with him dangled from his hand as he addressed the other two men. "The paramedics brought fifteen other people to this hospital yesterday. Some of them had to be admitted for overnight stays. Now, why don't you go and question some of them to see what they might have witnessed and get back to Jake later, when he might be more able to tell you something?''

Tracy stifled a sigh of relief, glad that she didn't have to be put in the sticky position of calling security to escort the policemen out, especially since, as with the Lone Star Country Club, some of the men who worked security here were off-duty policemen moonlighting at second jobs. There would be a decided conflict of interest.

Bancroft exchanged glances with Malloy. "He has a point.''

The older officer looked as if he needed little excuse to go off on Adam. He'd boxed while in the service and had progressed up through the ranks before he'd joined Stone's police force.

But after a moment, common sense prevailed and he relented with a shrug of his wide shoulders.

A resigned smile replaced the frown. "Okay, right." He looked at Adam. "I guess I got a little carried away, but the chief's been giving everyone a hard time about this thing happening on his watch and I just thought that since the boy was there—"

Adam cut him short. "You thought wrong." And then he allowed, "At least, for now."

"Sorry, kid, didn't mean to scare you." Malloy leaned over the bed in an attempt to seem concerned and friendly.

Jake's eyes shifted back to the ceiling.

"He's gonna come out of this, right?" Malloy asked Tracy.

She thought of what Lydia had told her this morning. "Hopefully. Time will tell, though."

This could be a break for all of them. If the kid remained like some stiff department-store dummy, it didn't matter what the hell he saw. Nobody would ever know.

"You mean there's a chance that he's going to stay like that?" he pressed the uppity witch in the white lab coat. "Like a zombie?"

Eager to withdraw, Bancroft took the lead. "Let's go, Kyle," he urged. He looked at Tracy. "Sorry to trouble you, Doctor. Maybe you can give us a call if and when the boy's up to talking." He took out a card and handed it to her.

This one, she thought, was at least trying to be decent. Tracy took the card, slipping it into her pocket after glancing at the officer's name. "I'll be sure to do that," she assured him.

Tracy turned to Adam as the two officers finally withdrew from the room. She had no idea that he was coming back, or what would have made him. But then, she wouldn't have thought a firefighter would stand out in the hall for over an hour, waiting to find out what happened to the boy he rescued, either.

She smiled at him, grateful for the timely arrival. "Is this the part where I flutter my eyelashes at you and call you my hero?"

He hadn't liked the way the other policeman had looked at her, as if she was just something for his amusement. And he definitely didn't like the way he was attempting to strong-arm her out of the way. Most of all, he hadn't wanted Jake to get upset.

It was a lot for Adam to digest about himself, seeing as he normally experienced the emotional involvement level of a piece of paper.

"You can do whatever you damn well like with your lashes, Doc," he told her. "I brought you something, kid." He placed a badly wrapped package on the boy's bed well within the boy's reach.

Jake continued staring at the ceiling.

Chapter 4

When Jake made no move to touch his gift, Adam picked up the package again.

"Maybe I'd better do this for you," he offered.

Keeping his eyes on the gift, feeling as if he were all thumbs, Adam began peeling off the heavily creased silvery wrapper he'd sealed around it not half an hour ago. He didn't know why he suddenly felt so self-conscious.

It was not the boy who made him feel awkward, but the woman standing off to the side, watching him.

He glanced up to see a smile on her face. "I'm not much at wrapping things," he mumbled.

"It's the thought that counts." Moving closer, she looked intently at the wrapper he'd just taken off. "Is that aluminum foil?"

"Yeah." He crumbled it quickly beneath his large hand. "I don't usually keep any wrapping paper around." When it came to occasions for his nieces and nephews, he usually left that up to his siblings, giving a generous check to cover whatever gift had caught the child's fancy. He hadn't wrapped anything since Bobby's fifth birthday. Doing so had brought back a flood of memories he had to bank down in order to finish sealing the gift.

"Very creative."

He hadn't a clue why the note of approval in her voice stirred him. But it did.

Still, he couldn't shake the growing feeling of being the proverbial bull in a china shop. Tossing out the foil, he held up the gift so that it was now in Jake's line of vision.

"It's a baseball glove," he finally told the boy when there was no reaction.

There was no indication from Jake that he'd even heard. His eyes remained fixed on the ceiling. Adam placed the glove back on the bed, beside the boy's hand. It didn't move. Only three fingers peeked out from beneath the bandage, the rest were hidden, swaddled along with his thumb and palm.

Adam looked at Tracy. Walking in, he'd only caught the last sentence of what was being said between her and the now departed policemen. "What's wrong with him?"

"He won't speak." Standing beside the bed, Tracy lightly brushed the thatch of blond hair from Jake's forehead. He was a good-looking little boy, with delicate features the fire hadn't etched its signature into. But it had branded more than the rest of his body. It had branded his soul. For how long? "It's his way of dealing with the trauma."

Adam wasn't into those kind of explanations. He firmly believed that his was a far less complex world that dealt with simple cause and effect. He searched for a more plausible explanation.

"Are you sure that he *can* talk?" His first thought was of damage done to the larynx. "I mean, he swallowed a lot of smoke before I got to him. Maybe—"

She knew what he was doing, what she'd done herself earlier. But she'd exhausted all other avenues looking for something to blame, something she could work with and hopefully fix.

This "fix" had to come from Jake.

Tracy shook her head, her hair falling into her face. She combed it back with her fingers.

"I've had tests done. There's nothing wrong with his larynx or his vocal chords, or his lungs," she added second-guessing his next suggestion as Adam opened his mouth again. "The injury goes deeper than anything we can readily fix." With a compassionate smile on her lips as she looked down at her small patient, she said softly, "The mind has ways of dealing with things that we can only guess at."

He hated coming up against things he couldn't control, couldn't set right. Exasperation chewed gaping holes in his chest. "So what'll it take to help him come out of it?"

Tracy sighed, sharing his feelings, wishing there was something more she could do. "Time, care—"

Adam looked at her sharply. He knew double-talk when he heard it. "In other words, you don't know."

She didn't attempt to snow him. Tracy sank her hands into her pockets. It would be so nice to be able to dig down deep and pluck out answers, she thought.

"In any words, I don't know. Not where I can give you a pat answer at any rate. We just have to wait and see." Her eyes shifted to the boy, smiling kindly at him. "Don't we, Jake?"

There was no reply. She didn't expect there to be.

Didn't seem fair, Adam thought. One second, the kid has the world on a string, everything to live for, the next, it all blows up on him.

Raising his head, Adam looked at Tracy. "I had someone check out his family."

He had been busy, she thought. Why did this boy mean so much to him? What was the connection? Was it just a case of a hero looking out for the person he rescued, or something more? In some cultures, she vaguely recalled, when you saved a life, it was yours forever to protect. Was there something like that going on here? She didn't know anything about this man, so it was hard to say.

"Oh?"

Damn, but it sounded as if there was a world of meaning in the way she said the one word, he thought. Probably just his imagination.

"He doesn't have one," he told her. "At least, none in the immediate area. Hell, none in the United States as far as I could find out. There's a second cousin or something like that." He saw immediate interest enter her eyes. Funny, he'd never thought of hazel eyes as being pretty before, but hers were. There were hints of bright green that shimmered at him and what looked to be flecks of sunshine. He roused himself and continued. "A Raymond Burke, but he's somewhere in Africa, dusting off old bones."

What an odd way to describe something. She tried to make sense of the encrypted words. "That means that Raymond Burke is either a dance instructor at an octogenarian social club, or he's—an anthropologist?"

Adam nodded. "The latter, although," he had to give her credit, "the first guess is pretty creative." His eyes washed over her, as if he was seeing her for the first time. Or going beyond the initial layer of an exceedingly attractive woman who looked way too young and vibrant to be someone's doctor. "A wise-cracking doctor with a pig who's not intimidated by the police. Pretty impressive."

She pressed her lips together, trying not to laugh, wondering if he realized that he'd made it sound as if Petunia was the one who faced officers of the law fearlessly. "I do my best."

The grin on her face faded into a soft smile he found too compelling. He looked away.

"It's nice of you to visit him," she finally said.

He shrugged. He'd never cared for attention directed his way. His mind scrambling, he said the first thing that occurred to him. "It's my day off. It's raining, so golf is out."

She tried to picture him on a driving range, sinking all his concentration into making a little round ball fly obediently through the air. The picture didn't materialize.

"You don't strike me as someone who golfs."

"I'm not," he confessed. Adam had no idea what had made him make that reference to golf. Probably because he'd seen scattered golf clubs on the green yesterday as he'd tried to resuscitate Jake. "Maybe some of your wisecracking's rubbing off."

The grin was back, shining in her eyes as she looked at him. "Maybe."

She wondered how he'd react if she asked him to grab a cup of coffee with her somewhere. There was something she wanted to run past him.

But just then, her beeper went off. With a sigh, she angled the small pager at her waist, trying to read the numbers on the LCD screen. She needn't have bothered. The telephone number was embossed on her brain.

"I'm wanted in emergency," she told him. Maybe it was just as well she didn't get a chance to ask, she thought. He'd probably turn her down and she didn't want Jake to overhear. Placing her hand lightly on the little boy's exposed fingers, she promised, "I'll see you in a little while, Jake." She was already backing out the door. "Nice seeing you again, Mr. Collins. Thanks for the rescue earlier."

She meant with the police, he realized. "Don't mention it." With the boy off in his own world, there was no reason to stay. Adam wasn't even sure that Jake knew he was in the room. "I guess I'd better be going myself."

Tracy paused in the doorway. She'd been hoping he'd remain. It was good for Jake. Even people in a coma sometimes responded to the presence of people in the room. Collins being here could only do Jake good.

"Oh, why don't you stay a little while?"

It wasn't a question, it was a request. Adam searched his brain for some kind of an excuse to give her, the awkward feeling beginning all over again. Absently, he pulled at the boy's blanket, straightening it.

As he started to say something about remembering a previous appointment that he'd made and forgotten about until just now, he felt the tips of Jake's fingers brush against his. Startled, wondering if he'd imagined it, Adam looked down at the bed.

Though he was still staring at the ceiling, Jake had wrapped his three fingers around Adam's hand. Just the way he had when he'd been placed on the gurney.

From out of nowhere, a large lump suddenly materialized and lodged itself in Adam's throat.

"Yeah," he muttered. Leaning, he pulled over a chair and sat down. He continued to hold the boy's three fingers in his hand. "Maybe I will." His voice lowered as he looked at Jake. "For a little while."

Smiling, relieved, Tracy quietly slipped out.

Bancroft and Malloy returned to the chief's office. They'd argued all the way from the hospital over the incident in the boy's room, each criticizing the other's approach. Bancroft had backed down. Malloy wasn't the kind to push too far.

Neither one of them had wanted to face the chief without an answer.

They drew straws and Malloy won. It was up to Bancroft to tell the chief.

Knocking on his superior's door, Bancroft waited until the latter growled for him to come in. When he did, he could feel the small, sharp darts coming at him from the man's steely blue eyes as Stone looked up from the preliminary task force report he was reading. There were red lines drawn through some of the sentences.

"Where's Malloy?" he wanted to know.

"Um, he had something to take care of." Bancroft summoned his flagging courage. His bad leg was bothering him again and he shifted his weight as subtly as possible. He knew the chief hated when he did that. "The boy's not talking, Chief."

Stone rose, staring incredulously at Bancroft. "What do you mean the boy's not talking?" he thundered. How the hell were they going to find out if the kid was a threat if they didn't know what he thought he saw? "*Make* him talk."

Bancroft shook his head frantically, knowing Stone had misunderstood him. "He can't. The lady doctor they've got watching the kid says it has something to do with his head."

Bancroft was two steps shy of being incoherent, Stone thought, aggravated. "Something wrong with his head?" he echoed. "Like what? Like he hit it?" the chief pressed impatiently. "Are you trying to tell me he's got some kind of amnesia?" Which he was undoubtedly faking, Stone was sure of it. Damn it all to hell, he was afraid of this. The kid knew something.

Again Bancroft shook his head, his thin, straggly

hair whipping about his ears like matted brown string. "No, he just doesn't talk. Stares up at the ceiling like his eyes are glued there."

Stone's eyes burned into him. "And you're buying this?"

Hesitating, Bancroft tried to read Stone's expression. He wasn't sure if the chief was testing him, baiting him or if he was asking a legitimate question. He tried to figure out how to convince Stone that he thought Jake was on the level.

"The kid never even blinked the entire time we were there."

A five-year-old staring off into space, that wasn't anything new or unusual. Suddenly needing a stiff drink, Stone settled on lighting up a cigar instead. Taking one out of the humidor on his desk, he bit off the end and spat it out. His eyes pinned Bancroft to the wall as he lit his cigar.

"What's the doctor say is wrong with him?"

Bancroft tried to remember if the woman had given the condition a name. She hadn't. "She calls it some kind of hysterical reaction."

"But it'll pass," Stone prodded.

If this was on the level, he qualified silently. And if it was, when it passed, the kid was sure to run off at the mouth about what he'd seen. Canvas bags stuffed with money. Money that El Jefe had sent and that painstakingly had been recorded, not once but twice in two sets of books, only one that would reach the drug lord. The other was for him so that he could keep track of exactly how much he had skimmed off the top before the money passed through the bank account he'd had set up here. The laundered funds then went back to their point of origin, representing investments in Emeralda, the import-export firm that comprised El Jefe's legitimate business holdings.

One slipup and it could all be over. He hadn't gotten where he was by leaving loose ends flapping in the breeze, loose ends that could undo him, Stone thought angrily.

Bancroft squirmed under the chief's heated glare. "We don't know."

Exasperated, Stone cursed at him roundly. "Well, who the hell does know?"

"Nobody," Bancroft replied helplessly. "She said it's just one of those things..."

Though the answers were infuriating him, Stone had no doubt that Bancroft was speaking the truth as he knew it. The man was too dumb, too frightened to lie.

"So's a noose if you catch my drift. I want you to stay close to the kid and check him out in another week or so. Ask around. If he so much as makes a peep or clears his throat, I want to know about it."

Damn, but this was frustrating. Stone knew what he would do if they were dealing with an adult. He'd have whoever it was terminated in the interest of the great cause. But this was a kid, and maybe a brain-damaged one at that, no matter what the doctor said. He didn't like the idea of eliminating a kid unless he had no other choice. He had kids of his own.

Which was part of what had gotten him into all this in the first place, he reminded himself angrily.

There were walls up no matter which way he

turned. Stone glared at the policeman. "You've got your assignment. Get out of my office," he ordered.

Bancroft didn't have to be told twice. He limped out quickly.

When she returned to Jake's room more than an hour later, Tracy was somewhat surprised to find Adam still there. The firefighter was sitting beside the boy's bed exactly as she'd left him, his hand extended over the railing, holding Jake's.

Adam's eyes shifted to her as she walked in.

Jake's eyes were closed and he looked to be asleep. "Your arm must be numb," she observed, lowering her voice.

It had gone past numb half an hour ago. "I can't feel my fingers," he confessed. Experiencing that same self-conscious feeling creeping over him again, he slowly eased his hand away from Jake's and then stood up. Adam wiggled his fingers slowly. They were stiff and it felt as if an army of ants were racing around inside his wrist. "There goes my tennis career."

Moving away from Jake's bed, she looked at Adam, amused. "I thought it was golf."

The shrug was dismissive, vague. "Whatever."

He wasn't an easy man to read. Tracy motioned Adam out into the hall and waited until he joined her just outside the glass enclosure around Adam's bed.

"You know, you don't have to be flippant about having a sensitive side."

He wasn't sure exactly what she was referring to and because he couldn't think of anything else to do,

Adam shrugged again. "I just thought the kid might like a baseball glove, that's all."

She was talking about him staying with Jake and holding his hand, about his coming to see the boy in the first place, but she allowed Adam the lie. "Did you at his age?"

The question brought back memories. He'd been short for his age, and a baseball glove seemed like a magic ticket into the world where all boys were momentarily created equal. "Hell, more than I wanted anything else in the whole world."

Tracy crossed her arms before her, her curiosity aroused. It wasn't easy visualizing him as a little boy Jake's age, but she tried. "Did you get one?"

"No." He recalled how hard he'd tried to hide his disappointment. Even then, he had been bent on hiding his emotions. "We couldn't afford it. My dad was laid off that year and every dime went to paying the rent and putting food on the table." He'd pretended it hadn't mattered to him. But it had. "There were seven of us."

"Seven." What was it like to have six brothers and sisters? she wondered. She would have felt lucky to have had one or two in her life, instead of being an only child. Like the Andersons, she realized. And Jake. "Lucky number."

He'd certainly never thought so. Neither had his parents, he was sure, though neither one had ever complained about the size of the family. They had just borne up to it, the two of them, doing what they needed to do in order to provide for the family.

"Two would have been luckier," he told her.

"Would have given my folks something in their pockets besides lint."

She understood what he was saying, but to her there was another criteria to measure by. "Money isn't everything."

Spoken like a woman who probably never had to do without, he thought cynically. He was willing to bet the petite, sexy doctor had never felt deprived of anything more important than tickets to a sold-out concert in her life. "It is when you don't have it."

She had been born into the lap of luxury. A luxury she eventually rejected, preferring to earn her own way. There was just her father now. Her mother had died when she was twenty-two. Try as she might, she couldn't remember either one of them ever truly being happy. "All the money in the world can't buy you happiness."

He would have loved his parents to have had the opportunity to discover that on their own. "Yeah, but it can sure eliminate the credit collectors that hassle you at all hours of the day and night."

Was he speaking from experience, or just pulling her leg? She thought of the upside of having a large family, something she'd once hoped to have herself. Before endometriosis had ended all her dreams. "Bet you had great Christmases, though."

Damn it, what did it take to make this woman's plane land? "I just told you, we were poor."

There was poor, and there was poor. In some ways, she knew she'd been poorer than he had been. "There were nine of you, counting your folks. You were rich,'' she told him firmly. ''Richer than Jake is right now.''

He began to say something to negate her assumption, then stopped. ''You're one of those Pollyanna types that turns people's stomachs, aren't you?''

She grinned. ''Guilty as charged, I'm afraid.''

''I had a feeling.''

Turning to look at him, she saw past the scowl on his face. ''Don't act as if you're some kind of Scrooge because I won't believe you.''

Definitely a stomach turner, he thought. ''Not that I care what you believe, but why not?''

That was so easy, it hardly bore stating. ''Because if you were one, you wouldn't have turned up today. And you wouldn't have waited around yesterday to find out how he was doing.''

She had a smug expression curving her mouth. Adam found himself wanting to wipe it off. With his own. Surprised, he blocked out the thought. When he spoke, his tone was curt, cold, as he tried to verbally push her away.

''I told you, I pulled him out of the fire. I like knowing if I risked my neck for nothing.''

''That sounds very cold and callous.'' But it didn't fool her for a minute.

His eyes narrowed. Was she finally getting it? ''It is.''

''But you're not,'' she told him. There was no room for argument in her tone. ''Why are you trying to convince yourself that you are?''

He had better things to do than go head-to-head

with a stubborn woman with curly black hair. "I didn't come here to be analyzed."

The smile she flashed undulated its way inside him, like a chance encounter with rays of sunshine on an overcast day. He tried to shake off the reaction.

"Consider it a freebie."

What he considered it—and her—to be was a giant pain in the butt. "I thought burns were your specialty, not shrinking heads."

"I branched out a little." He looked as if he was about to take off. Not wanting him to leave just yet, she changed tactics. "Seriously, I'm glad you came to see him."

He didn't see why his visit mattered one way or another. "A lot of good it did."

"Oh, but it did," she insisted. How could he think that it didn't? "I saw Jake take your hand. That's the most response I've seen out of him since they brought him in."

He still found it difficult to wrap his mind around the fact that Jake hadn't spoken to anyone, hadn't said anything.

"And he really hasn't said a word? Not to anyone?" Adam asked incredulously.

"Not a single word." Though she was trying not to dwell on it, it really concerned her. "Not even a whimper after you brought him in, and I know he was in pain. Painkillers wear off."

Adam stared through the glass at the still form lying in the bed. "How long do you think he'll have to stay here?"

"Well, his parents had a great insurance plan so

there's no rush for his bed." It was the side of healing she hated, reckoning with the demands of insurance companies—all the red tape and paperwork that ultimately threatened to dehumanize patients.

He didn't quite understand. "The insurance was his father's, right?"

"Right."

"But his father's dead." Didn't that mean that the policy was terminated?

She knew what he was thinking. It was a common misconception. "Doesn't matter, it goes to the end of the month, or, in the event of a dependent's hospital confinement when the insured dies, the coverage continues until after the patient is discharged."

It seemed like little enough compensation for Jake's loss. "So he has a little leeway?"

"Yes, luckily."

Adam looked at the boy again, feeling his heart twist in his chest. Damn, but he looked like Bobby. "But eventually, he has to be discharged."

"Well, yes, he can't stay in the hospital indefinitely."

He continued his thought. "To social services."

She didn't like it any more than he did. "They'd be handling his case."

Though he had led his life these last two years trying to distance himself from everything and anything, he still didn't like the dehumanized way of looking at Jake's situation.

"He doesn't have a case, he has a life," Adam said sharply.

Tracy took a step back, surprised by his tone.

"Hey, don't jump all over me. I'm not the one who set the bomb and destroyed innocent lives."

She was right, it wasn't her fault. He had no right to yell at her. "Sorry, I don't usually lose my temper like that."

Because he apologized, she let it slide. "What do you usually do?"

What he should have done in this case, he told himself. "Not pay attention to things."

"But this is different." It wasn't a question. It was an observation. One that applied to both of them, she thought, because somehow, it was different for her as well. Jake was alone and she couldn't bear the thought of that.

"Yes, this is different."

Wheels began to turn in her head. She remembered what she'd wanted to ask him when her pager had gone off. "I suppose, if you feel that strongly about it, maybe I can talk to a friend of mine who's in social services. She might be able to pull some strings to allow you to have temporary custody of the boy."

His head whipped around and he stared at her incredulously. "Me?"

He sounded stunned. "I'm sorry, did I misunderstand something? I thought you were volunteering."

"Well, I wasn't. I was just being concerned." Frustrated, Adam searched for the right words. "Look, I can't take him in. I'm a firefighter. On two days, off two days."

Tracy was well aware of the schedule. "Maybe your wife—"

He cut her off curtly. "I don't have a wife."

"Then why—?" Her eyes automatically went to the plain gold band on his left hand. "I'm sorry, I'm not trying to pry into your private life, it's just that you're wearing a wedding ring, so I thought—"

He was going to have to get better control over himself than this, he thought. That's three times he'd bitten her head off. "My wife died two years ago. I just wasn't ready to take it off."

Moved by the traces of sorrow echoing in his voice despite his obvious effort to mute them, Tracy laid her hand on his. She hadn't meant to unearth anything painful. "I'm sorry, really sorry."

Given the nature of her work, he knew that she had to say those words a dozen times a month if not more.

But the thing of it was, he believed her.

Chapter 5

Adam had no idea what had come over him. Why he was standing here in the middle of a hospital, telling this strange woman things he didn't readily talk about with either his siblings or the people he knew and worked with.

Things that were locked away in his soul.

Maybe there was something to the idea that it was easier to talk to a stranger than to someone who was actually a part of your life. And maybe seeing Jake this way had triggered it, bringing back a flood of memories Adam had struggled for two years to contain if not blot out altogether.

Yet Adam didn't want to share this, not with this efficient, effervescent lady doctor who was too optimistic for her own good. Not with anyone. Didn't want to touch upon things that after all this time, could still slice through him like a newly sharpened hunting knife.

Hearing her express sorrow at his loss didn't help mute the feeling.

"Yeah," he murmured in response to her condolences, "me, too."

He looked at her. Tracy had begun by suggesting something that he'd actually entertained himself earlier today. Hearing it said aloud had made him momentarily feel as if he were being put on the spot, but in reality, he hadn't really liked the idea of Jake being placed in a foster home.

Adam supposed the idea of taking him in wasn't really such a stretch.

He blew out a breath, "Look, maybe something can be arranged and I can take Jake in until this second cousin can be found and checked out." He paused, thinking. There were logistics involved here. "I'll have to get someone to stay with the boy on the days that I'm working at the station."

Maybe Tina, one of his sisters-in-law, could be persuaded to take the boy in, he thought. It would require some rescheduling, but nothing that couldn't be done. Tina was great with kids and a pushover for a hard luck story.

Tracy studied him as he spoke, making up her mind. If this solemn, stoic man could find it in his heart to try to aid a child in need, then the least she could do was help him.

"If you can tell me your schedule ahead of time, I could see about having mine arranged so that I can cover for you on the days when you're working."

God knew she had enough leverage to be able to do that, Tracy thought. Ever since she'd discovered that she'd unwittingly allowed her case of endometriosis to go untreated until it was too late and she could never have the children she so desperately craved, Tracy had thrown herself into her work. She'd taken on double shifts, worked an enormous amount of overtime and volunteered to cover for other people when they couldn't come in. She'd accrued so much extra time that she knew she could easily cull this favor from the head attending physician in the E.R.

His gaze held her suspect. He wasn't accustomed to people volunteering to help, especially someone who didn't know him. "Why would you do that?"

Her mouth curved in a half smile. "Maybe for the same reason you are."

Adam shook his head. "No. I don't think so."

He was doing it because Jake reminded him of Bobby. Because Bobby was gone and he hadn't been able to save him, but he had saved Jake. Because he had lost a son and the mother of his child and Jake had lost a father and a mother. It gave the two of them a great deal in common, a loss they could bond over, even if nothing was ever said to acknowledge it. The woman standing next to him knew none of this, and, unless he missed his guess, had none of this in her own life.

Whatever her reasons were, they weren't his.

He was being uncommunicative again, Tracy thought, but she let it pass. She didn't want to argue, she wanted to help.

"All right. Then let's say I'm doing it because I

love kids and I think that Jake has enough to deal with without having to go through the trauma of being passed from hand to hand in social services.'' Tracy leaned against the glass, for the moment her back to the boy whose life they were both concerned about. ''What he needs at this moment is time to heal. From the inside out. Being placed in a foster home might not be the best thing for him right now and to be fair, you can't expect someone to just be able to jump in and handle his special needs at a time like this. Being a pediatric doctor gives me a slight edge in that department.''

She waited for Adam to say something. When he didn't, she pressed, ''So, is it a deal?''

He didn't see why she was asking him. ''You've probably got more of a say in this than I do, seeing as how he's on your turf.''

You're a strange, strange man, Adam Collins. What makes you tick? Her smile was engaging. ''That's okay, I've never been known to throw my weight around.''

There was something about her smile that seemed to cut through the layers of sadness that were wrapped so tightly, so permanently, around his soul. For a second, Adam stopped resisting and just allowed the warmth that her smile generated to come through.

''I'll remember that,'' he told her.

It sounded like a promise, but she knew it wasn't. The man was just making conversation, nothing more. Tracy glanced at her watch. It was getting close to noon. ''Well, I have rounds to make.''

He nodded, part of him relieved that she was leaving. "I think I'll stick around a little longer, be here in case he wakes up."

To look at the man, one would have never guessed that he possessed this softer side. Just shows you could never tell, she mused.

"You're one of the good guys, Collins."

Impulsively, Tracy raised herself up on her toes and brushed her lips against his cheek. Adam jerked, as if she'd touched a match to his flesh, and looked at her in complete surprise. Tracy backed up, though her smile didn't fade. *First time that ever happened.*

"Don't worry," she told him. "It washes off."

Adam stood in the hall and watched the trim woman hurry off down the corridor, feeling just a little more human than he had a moment ago and not altogether sure just why.

Tracy took to stopping by Jake's room whenever she had a free moment. She was determined to treat not only his burns, but his other wounds as well. She brought him games, located cartoon videos for him to watch and carried on conversations with him as if he were giving her answers instead of silence.

Patience was her main weapon. She'd learned it early on. When she was eight years old, she'd taken a bad spill off a sled and spent the next year learning how to walk all over again. The physical therapist her parents had hired had been a matronly-looking woman named Olga. Olga wore her hair tightly wound around her head in a thick, faded blond braid, had a Swedish accent that could easily have been sliced with a knife and possessed the gentlest touch

Tracy had ever encountered. Though the sessions were grueling and painful, Olga never once allowed her to give up, even when she begged.

It was thanks to Olga that she walked now without a limp. More than that, the woman had taught her patience and that important things always took a long time to accomplish.

It was also at the age of eight that Tracy first fell in love with medicine and ultimately found her calling. She wanted to help others the way she'd been helped. If it hadn't been for the quick action of the emergency room physician who'd relieved the pressure building up on her spine, she later discovered, she might never have been able to walk again, period. As she had lain, convalescing, she had made a deal with God. If he allowed her to walk again, she would find a way to make that kind of a difference in other children's lives.

It was a promise she didn't forget. It was a promise she wanted to act on now.

"It's a bad idea, Trace."

Maureen Ryan, one of the nurses in the E.R. and her best friend, sat looking at her over a cup of lukewarm coffee in the hospital cafeteria. She was specifically referring to what Tracy had just told her she intended to do about the boy who had been brought in with his own personal firefighter.

Time and again, Maureen had seen Tracy give more than a hundred and ten percent for one of her patients. But this went beyond that.

She knew Tracy's heart was in the right place, but Maureen despaired about the location of her friend's common sense. More to the point, that it seemed to be missing in action.

"Maybe the first name's the same, Trace, but you really just can't keep trying to be Mother Teresa to the whole world."

She knew Maureen meant well, but Maureen didn't understand what drove her. Maureen had three kids of her own. She didn't know what it meant to face a life that stretched out before her, childless.

"Not the whole world, Maureen," Tracy told her. "It's just one small boy."

It was far more than that and they knew it. It was getting involved above and beyond the call. "I've heard about taking your work home with you but this is carrying things a little too far." Maureen leaned forward, keeping her voice down, but not her attempt to talk some sense into Tracy. "Look, you're doing what you're supposed to be doing, honey. You're making sure the burns heal correctly. Let social services do its job when the time comes."

"But you've seen him, Maureen. Most of the time he just stares off into space." Once or twice, she'd gotten him to acknowledge her presence, to look her way when she spoke, but for the most part, he was withdrawn.

Maureen sighed, knowing that this was a futile effort. "My point exactly. You're a burn specialist, not a psychiatrist."

"I'm a human being first, Maureen." She paused, then added, "And I'm not doing this alone."

Interest entered Maureen's green eyes. "You mean Mr. Hot Stuff's in on it?" For the first time since

Tracy had told Maureen her plans, a smile appeared on her friend's generous mouth. "Well, now that makes more sense." She nodded her wholehearted approval.

Caught up in what she intended to do, Maureen's reference eluded her at first. "What are you talking about?"

The handsome, silent firefighter was all the talk on the pediatric floor. "Hey, I've seen the man sitting in the room with the boy." Maureen pretended to fan herself, rolling her eyes. "My-oh-my, he can light my fire any day. If he's going to be helping you, then by all means, go for it. You have my blessings, girl," she added with a deep chuckle.

Though she wasn't about to argue that Adam Collins was definitely an attention grabber, Tracy didn't want the wrong story about her motives getting around. Though she loved Maureen dearly, as far as Maureen was concerned, the word "silence" meant lowering her voice to a whisper. She wanted Maureen to understand that this was strictly about the boy.

"I'm not going for anything. And Collins is the one taking the boy in, not me. I just volunteered to pick up the slack and be with the boy the days Collins is on duty."

Maureen's dark eyebrows rose comically. "And the nights?"

Tracy thought that was understood. After all, the man was a firefighter and firefighters were supposed to be at the station around the clock when they were on. "Yes, the nights, too."

One look at Tracy told Maureen they weren't talking about the same thing. She shook her head, her dark, curly hair moving from side to side like thousands of tiny, bouncy springs. All this dedication seemed to have completely eroded Tracy's libido, she thought in mounting concern.

"No, I mean the nights that Mr. Delicious Firefighter's home."

Tracy looked at her innocently. "The nights he's home, there'll be no need for me to be there, will there? I'll be here, making up my time."

"You're deliberately toying with me, aren't you?"

"Maureen, what's important here is the boy—"

"Yes, I understand that, believe me." Leaning forward again, she pressed a hand to her breast. "I feel for that child. But I feel for you, too, Tracy. You've been alone too long, girl. It's not natural. And there's nothing that says you can't be rewarded for being a good Samaritan now, is there?" Her expression became mischievous, sensual. "Maybe reward each other?"

This clearly wasn't getting her anywhere. Maureen looked at Tracy in exasperation. "How long *has* it been since you were on a date?"

Tracy shrugged noncommittally. It wasn't anything she kept track of. "I don't remember."

Sympathy entered Maureen's black eyes. "That long, eh?"

She was doing something good. The last thing she wanted was pity, especially about something so trivial. "This isn't about dating."

Maureen's chuckle was deep, rich, like the color of

her hair. "No, it's about getting some. You haven't been and you should."

It wasn't that she didn't want to see men, it was that she was too busy. Besides, what was the point? To her, the reason behind the whole experience of love and marriage was to have a family. For her that was medically impossible. "Do you think a happily married woman should be talking like this?"

They'd been friends for three years and Maureen felt she was closer to Tracy than anyone. It gave her the right to pry, to nudge.

"Who better? Look, you're the noblest person who ever walked the face of the earth and I admire you for it, but all work and no play makes Tracy—"

"Dedicated," Tracy supplied.

"That wasn't the word I was going for." She placed her hand over Tracy's in mute support, her expression earnest. "Honey, just because you can't have kids doesn't mean you can't play house. This is a perfect opportunity to do it—just as long as you don't get too attached to the boy."

Or the man.

Tracy caught herself up short. Where had that come from? Undoubtedly, from Maureen's badgering. Draining her cup, Tracy placed it on the tray and squared her shoulders. "I appreciate the concern, but why don't you let me worry about that?"

Maureen knew her better than that. "But you won't, so I'm your designated worrier."

Tracy laughed, shaking her head. She rose from the table and picked up the tray. "I've got to get going."

"Keep me posted," Maureen called after her. "I need a fantasy life."

Tracy looked at her over her shoulder. "You're married."

A wide grin split Maureen's even wider face. "Like I said, I need a fantasy life."

She always got in the last word, Tracy thought as she walked away. But not the last thought. This *was* just about Jake and handsome though Mr. Tall, Dark and Silent was, that had no bearing on what she was doing.

Adam listened to the voice on the other end of the line. He nodded, though the woman couldn't see him. It was a done deal. For the next month at least, Jake Anderson was his.

There was a flutter in his stomach. Oh God, what had he done?

Annoyed with himself, with what he deemed as a selfish and self-centered reaction, he locked the uncertainty away. What he had done was to reach out to a boy who badly needed someone in his corner. Since the boy had made it clear in his own fashion that he had singled him out, the least he could do was to be there for Jake.

Foster's sister had gone out on a limb and pulled every string she had available to her. The end result was that Jake was his to care for. Temporarily. "Thanks, Jenny. I appreciate everything you've done. I owe you and your brother, big time."

"You don't owe me anything," the soft voice assured him. "Just take good care of Jake. Someone

from social services will be by to look in on the two
of you. With any luck, it'll be me, but it might not.
Rules,'' she explained.

"I understand."

"Good luck."

He could hear the woman's well-intentioned smile.
''Thanks.''

God knew he was going to need it. Adam hung up,
blowing out a long, calming breath. He was taking on
a hell of a lot. It was quite a change from his lifestyle.
In the past two years, outside of the job he'd kept to
himself, interacting with no one. Now he was going
to have a little boy to care for. A little boy who was
shut away in his own private hell, either by choice or
design, but it didn't alter the fact that Jake was going
to need kid-glove care.

He didn't know if he was up to it. But the image
of Jake, lying on the gurney, clutching his hand,
wouldn't let him back out. There'd been a mute appeal for help in those huge blue eyes the boy had
turned on him. Adam knew that if he walked away
now, he would never have any peace. He had no
choice but to take the boy in. His conscience had left
him no leeway.

He'd been stopping by the hospital on his days off
this last week, hoping to somehow break through to
the boy. Jake was walking now, albeit haltingly because of the burns to his legs. The first time he'd
witnessed Jake's therapy, saw the pain in the boy's
eyes, he'd almost told the therapist to stop. But he
knew that would be the worst thing to do. It was
essential that Jake exercise his limbs to keep the skin

from shrinking and tightening as it healed, to keep his muscles from atrophying. Otherwise, his legs were in danger of withering. Adam had seen it happen.

It was painful to watch, but Adam forced himself to be there for the boy. If Jake could put up with it, so could he.

The therapist, Randi, a ponytailed, perky blonde whose bounciness was second only to Tracy's, had instructed him on what to do when he'd asked. She seemed impressed that he was interested, but Adam felt he was going to need to be able to help Jake with the exercises once the boy came home with him. He wanted to help the boy recover. Otherwise, he felt he'd have done Jake more harm than good, saving him.

Adam had watched Randi and the boy intently, making mental notes even though he had a backup system in place. He assumed that Tracy would know what to do in case he forgot or got it wrong.

As he stood there, watching, the day before Jake's release, he became aware of the change that had come about. Not with Jake, but within him.

When had he stopped thinking of her as the doctor and started thinking of her as Tracy?

He wasn't sure.

Probably around the time she'd stood outside the boy's room and kissed him.

Adam wondered vaguely now, as he drove to the hospital to pick the boy up, what it would be like to kiss Tracy. Not just fleetingly, or on the cheek, but really kiss her. The way a man kissed a woman.

Not that he planned to, but it didn't hurt anything

to idly wonder about it. In a way, he supposed it was a good sign. Showed that he wasn't completely dead inside, as he'd surmised he was all this time.

But the very next moment, there was a deep, penetrating flash of guilt spearing his soul. He hadn't so much as looked at another woman since Gloria had died. Gloria had been his high school sweetheart. Hell, she'd been his girl since the eighth grade. He couldn't even recall dating anyone else, ever. He'd known Gloria was the one for him ever since he'd first seen her.

Which made him feel disloyal, he told himself, to even remotely entertain idle thoughts about kissing Jake's doctor.

He blew out a breath as he approached the parking lot. When had things become this damn complicated? All he'd ever wanted was a simple life. Marry the girl he'd always loved, have a couple of kids and someday, retire. Maybe go fishing like his dad had done with him and his brothers. Not exactly an extraordinary plan.

Except that for him, it had been. For him a fire that had broken out in his home because of faulty wiring in a walk-in closet had wiped out in a heartbeat what had been so dear to his heart.

He hadn't believed the call when it came into the station house. Hearing his own address recited back to him initially had all but paralyzed him. His heart had been lodged in his throat the entire ten minutes it had taken for the fire truck to barrel out of the station and arrive at his house.

There'd been nothing to save.

The house was almost entirely engulfed in flames and although he'd raced in, shouting their names, he knew he was already too late. Gloria and Bobby were already dead, dying of smoke inhalation before the fire ever got to them.

He supposed he should be grateful for that, that they hadn't suffered.

Only he suffered.

And continued to suffer.

With a start, he realized that he'd reached the hospital. It took some effort, but he shook off his thoughts as he parked his car. It was time to think about someone other than himself.

Adam got out of the car and walked to the hospital entrance.

Chapter 6

Bonnie Brannigan's three-inch heels clicked rhythmically on the deep, rich red Spanish tile as she quickly approached the uniformed policeman who was about to walk away. He had just made his exit from behind the yellow-taped, padlocked makeshift pine enclosure that separated the fire-gutted area that had so recently been the popular Men's Grill from the rest of the Lone Star Country Club, proclaiming it a crime scene. Trespassers were forbidden.

Afraid he would get away before she could speak to him, she stepped up her pace, swaying provocatively as she tottered from side to side. Unable to reach the police chief by phone, Bonnie had been waiting for someone official to show up at the club for days. Bonnie had a key to the padlock, but a key didn't answer the question that needed to be addressed.

"Um, excuse me." Her appeal didn't seem to register. The policeman kept on walking. Bonnie raised her voice. "Excuse me, Officer?"

The stocky man turned around. Malloy's deep-set gray eyes took quick measure of the woman, taking in the mature, still shapely figure, the platinum hair piled high on her head and the crimson-outlined smile. He took in, too, the way her pink sweater adhered to her breasts, moving with every breath she took.

This had to be the Lone Star Country Club's general manager the chief had told him about.

No problem, he thought. He could definitely handle her. Taking a stance that was part patient, part authoritative, he looked at her with reserved politeness. "Yes, ma'am?"

"Oh, Bonnie, please," she insisted. A Texan, born and bred, she still hated the way "ma'am" sounded. It made her feel years older than she liked to think she looked. "Bonnie Brannigan," she clarified, extending her slim hand to him. When he shook it, her charm bracelet jangled melodiously. Bonnie smiled up at him warmly, just the way her mama had taught her. *Men are like putty in a pretty girl's hand, Sugar. Always remember that.* Up until now, Mama had been right. "I'm the general manager here and I was just wondering when you boys were going to unwrap all of this."

"Ma'am?"

"Bonnie," she repeated a tad more forcefully. She waved a hand at the enclosure which looked so out of place in the lavish country club. "Take down that awful door and the pine wall with it. I truly do need to start renovations going here, Officer Malloy," she purred, reading the name on his badge. "I'm afraid this awful-looking area is making the club members feel uneasy," she confided, leaning in to him. "They come here to relax, not to worry that they might be blown to little tiny bits as they're strolling by or teeing off on the range."

She took a long breath, sighing, as if she fully understood how taxing and important his work was.

"I truly don't mean to rush you, but..." She glanced over his shoulder at what had once been her favorite place within the club. "Have you been able to find anything yet? I mean, like clues?"

Malloy had no idea if the chief had formulated what to tell the press and the people in charge of the club yet, or which of the various speculations that the public at large was making he wanted to validate. Rumors were growing and changing almost daily and it was hard to keep up. As far as he knew, Stone was playing all of this close to the chest.

"We've found lots of clues, ma'am." Most of which had been systematically swept away by certain chosen members of the task force, whose job it was not to find clues but to eliminate them. "But there are no official answers yet."

"Oh," Bonnie declared, her eyes growing bright. "You've got a pin like mine." To illustrate, she held up her overburdened charm bracelet and shook her hand so that it jingled loudly. She found the lion pin she'd converted into a charm and pointed it out. "The mayor gave me mine for outstanding service,'' she said proudly, starting to reach out to touch his pin.

Malloy pulled back, not wanting her to look closely. The woman might notice that while they appeared to be completely alike at first glance, on closer scrutiny the two pins were just a shade different. On his the lion's leg that was partially hidden behind the other three was broken off.

IIc wanted to get going. He'd only come by to make certain that nothing at the crime scene had been disturbed. One of the security people had discovered that his pin was missing and Stone wanted to be certain it wouldn't turn up at the bombing site.

''I'll take your concerns up with Chief Stone the next time I see him,'' Malloy promised.

''Oh, please do. And be sure to give him my regards, will you, Officer Malloy?'' she asked prettily. ''Tell him I know he's doing a fine job and I don't mean to rush him, but—''

It sounded as if she was going to launch into her explanation all over again. Malloy didn't want to stay for a second performance. He had this feeling in his gut that the woman could go on and on. He had no time to stand here and placate her.

''I'll be sure to tell him,'' he said quickly interrupting her. He tipped his Stetson hat. ''Be seeing you, ma'am.''

What a strange man, Bonnie mused, watching him walk away. If she didn't know better, she would have said he was trying to avoid her questions. But that was silly. He was just probably very busy. After all, if you couldn't trust the police, who could you trust?

She just wished they'd hurry up and find out who was responsible for all this so that life could get back to normal.

What a pity life couldn't be like it was in those TV crime shows her fiancé, C.J., liked so much. Everything done up in a neat, tidy package in just under an hour, if you didn't count the commercials.

She sighed, and shook her head as she looked back at the pine wall that hid the charred remains of the Grill. Something had to be done about this, and soon. It just couldn't remain in this horrible condition.

She wrinkled her nose. The smell of smoke still clung to the air even after two weeks.

Tracy had made a point of getting people to cover for her this morning. Making sure all shifts were spoken for, she was free to take the day off. She came into Jake's room in her official capacity as his doctor only insofar as it was necessary in order to sign the boy out, which she did.

Off duty for the first time in almost a year, she was ready to help Adam out with the boy in any way she could. Though she hadn't run it by him, she felt he was going to need her. This was going to be Jake's first day in a different environment, some place other than the hospital, and she had a feeling the boy would be agitated. She figured Adam could use the backup.

She'd checked Jake's vital signs and noted down his present condition as part of signing him out of the hospital. The wounds were healing far faster than she'd expected and she was well pleased.

"A year from now," she told Jake cheerfully as

she helped him dress, "there'll hardly be any marks left on your body from the burns." She smiled up at him brightly. "I think that's pretty good news, don't you?"

Jake said nothing, but then that was now normal for him. She'd made up her mind almost from the start to keep up a steady stream of conversation whenever she was around Jake in the hopes that eventually he would actually reply.

"Big day for you, huh?" She gently pulled up one sock on his foot. "Going home with Adam. You know, he had to talk to a lot of people to get their okay before he was allowed to take you home with him. There're a lot of people out there who care what happens to you, Jake."

The boy needed to know this and to have it reinforced as many times as she could bring it into the conversation. He'd lost the two people whose love he had taken for granted would always be there. It had shaken the foundations of his world and she knew that it was going to be slow going before he allowed someone else in, believing that they loved him.

She took out the second sock and put it on his foot. "I know it might not feel that way to you right now, but there are. There's Adam, and Randi and me, of course, plus a whole bunch of other people whose job it is to make sure little boys like you find some place with a nice, loving family to look out for them."

She stopped for a moment, trying to make eye contact with the boy. He seemed to be staring straight through her, as if she were clear as glass. As if she weren't there. She took both of his hands in hers, shifting her head until she thought she saw his eyes flicker in her direction.

"Are you in there, Jake?" she asked softly. "Can you hear anything I'm saying? It's okay not to talk, okay if you just want to be your own best buddy right now, but I want you to know that we're here for you when you're ready for us. Adam and I, we're here."

Hand on the door as he opened it, the force of Tracy's words hit Adam with the precision of a bullet fired dead on target.

About to enter the room, Adam stopped.

Adam and I.

It made them sound as if they were a set, as if he and this exuberant lady doctor with the quick smile and easy laugh belonged together. But they didn't. All they were were two people interested in the same little boy, hoping for the same end goal: to have the boy come back around to the world of the living.

There was nothing else.

Adam walked in, letting the door close noisily behind him. He saw Tracy turn and look at him. She wasn't wearing her white lab coat, he noted, wondering why. Every other time he'd seen her, she'd had it on, the sides flapping around her trim figure as she walked.

Seeing her dressed in civilian clothing made things different somehow. She didn't look like a doctor, all cool, competent and collected. She looked, instead, like a woman. A gut-wrenchingly attractive woman who looked as if she could be at ease in almost any circumstance, in any setting.

That put her one up on him.

He was here to bring Jake home, Adam silently upbraided himself, not to wax poetic—and badly so—about a woman he hardly knew.

Adam crossed to the bed where the boy was sitting on top of the covers. "Hi, Jake. You ready yet?"

"Just about," Tracy answered for the silent boy. "Just need to get our shoes on." Kneeling down in front of him, she slipped on the first athletic shoe. Though she knew it wasn't easy because of the burns, Jake held his foot perfectly still.

Adam felt compelled to make conversation. Standing over Tracy this way, so close to her, made him lose his concentration.

He looked at Jake. "Hey, neat footwear." He infused enthusiasm in his voice. "Who got those for you?"

Tracy made a large, loopy bow as she tied off the laces on the right shoe. "I did." She picked up the other one and smiled at Jake as if he'd said something instead of merely staring off, oblivious to the exchange. "They're going to help you run like the wind once you start hitting those homers, aren't they, Jake?"

The boy sat on the bed, letting her put on the other shoe, his gaze fixed on some invisible spot on the wall behind her head.

Adam sank his hands deep into the pockets of his blue jeans. He wondered if he was up to this, if he could somehow find the key that would unlock this boy's prison and bring Jake back into the world he had once inhabited. Or did sentimentality have him biting off more than he could chew?

Tracy rose to her feet, dusting off her hands. She saw the expression on Adam's face. "Second thoughts?" she guessed.

"No." The response was quick, automatic. Being anything but certain was not the way he wanted to be perceived, especially when Tracy appeared so damnably optimistic and upbeat.

"That's good." She picked up the boy's jacket and began to slip it on his arms. "Okay, I think we're ready to go, aren't we, Jake?"

Adam had a feeling something was going on here that hadn't been run by him first. "Is that the editorial 'we'?"

Their eyes locked. It hadn't occurred to her that Adam might not welcome her help. Maybe it should have, Tracy now thought. There was something very guarded in his tone.

"No, that's the encompassing 'we,' as in 'you and me.'" She pointed to Jake and then herself to underline her meaning. "And you as well, since it's your house."

"Apartment," he corrected, still looking at her. Something told him that he should have seen this coming. And that maybe, all things considered, it wasn't such a bad thing, anyway. "Are you telling me, in your unique, roundabout style, that you're coming with us?"

She cocked her head, amused. Her whole focus had been on getting through to Jake. Maybe she would take a crack at piercing Adam's shell as well while she was at it.

A smile curved along her lips like misty smoke.

She was putting him on the spot and she knew it. "You really think I'm unique?"

"That's one word for it," he allowed. One of a kind also came to mind as a description. "You didn't answer my question. Are you coming with us?"

Tracy nodded. "Yes. I thought you two might need a little help the first day out. You know, adjusting," she added.

Adam started to tell her that he didn't need help, that he and the boy would do fine on their own, but then he thought better of it. Because it was a lie. They just might not do fine at all. The truth of it was that he was probably going to need help with this transition and she seemed to be a lot better with kids than he was. Hell, he thought, a mannequin was probably better with kids than he was.

Besides, he hadn't asked her to, she was volunteering. That made a difference.

"Not a bad thought," he told her.

The smile that glimmered on her lips hit him like a burst of sunshine before he had a chance to prepare himself.

"Is that a compliment, Collins?"

"If you want it to be," he finally said guardedly. Not wanting her to make too much of it, he advised, "Don't let it go to your head."

"Wouldn't dream of it." Her attention shifted to the boy sitting so stoically on the bed. Jake was wearing a baseball cap one of the nurses had given him to hide his partially singed hair and there were still bandages on his arms as well as on his legs beneath the baggy trousers Tracy had carefully slipped on him. "Ready for your new adventure, Jake?"

Silent, Jake allowed her to gently lift him from the bed, her hands carefully placed where the damage from the flames had been minimal.

"Adventure," Adam echoed. "Is that what we call it now?" He should have known she'd call it something whimsical like that. The term would never have occurred to him.

Tracy nodded. "Everything's an adventure if you just keep the right perspective."

He didn't know whether to label her pushy, or just exuberant. He decided to withhold judgment. "Meaning yours?"

She half-shrugged. "My perspective is always optimistic," she explained, though she knew it was needless. That man had undoubtedly picked up on that. "Works for me."

She was young, beautiful and intelligent, with her whole life in front of her: a long career, a family, everything was still waiting in the wings for her. She had something to be optimistic about, he thought.

It was different for him. Most of his life was behind him. Irrevocably lost.

But in light of the fact that he was now, however temporarily, in charge of the young life he had rescued, Adam knew he was going to have to try to restructure his way of thinking, at least for the time being.

For Jake's sake.

"I guess it is an adventure at that," he said to the boy. "Well, you ready to go on your 'adventure'?"

Knowing there would be no answer, he reached for the boy's hand to lead him to the wheelchair that was waiting for him. The hospital mandated that everyone being discharged was to be escorted out in this fashion.

In Jake's case, Adam thought it seemed especially advisable since he had no idea how far the boy's strength would take him if he attempted to walk out. Tracy seemed to have no problem picking him up, but it was a long way from here to the entrance if measured in steps and he was afraid that he might hurt the boy if he attempted to carry him out. He couldn't see himself doing anything but placing his hands on all the wrong places.

Rather than allow Adam to take his hand, Jake pulled back.

"Hey, buddy, what's up? Don't you want to come with me?" Adam asked in the friendliest voice he could summon. Jake didn't look at him. Instead, in response, Jake looked around the room. "Is he afraid to leave?" Adam asked Tracy, completely at a loss.

She was about to tell Adam that she honestly didn't know when she saw Jake look toward the shelf that ran along the side wall by the sink. The boy's expression suddenly relaxed as his eyes came to rest on the object lying there.

Moving around the bed, Tracy crossed to the shelf. "No, he just doesn't want to go without his glove, do you Jake?" Picking it up, she handed it to the boy who took it and held it against his chest.

Minor breakthrough number one. She raised her

eyes and looked at Adam, her smile warm. "Looks like you're on the right track, Collins."

"Glad one of us thinks so," he murmured. "Okay, ready, Jake? Didn't forget anything else, did we?"

Tracy did a final sweep of the room. The boy had no possessions of his own, only those things others had given him during his stay here. A St. Jude medal hung around his neck, courtesy of Randi, the physical therapist whose heart he had won, and his clothes had come from Maureen, whose own son Isaac was a year older than Jake and had outgrown the pants and T-shirt Jake was now wearing. The shoes and parka jacket she now slipped onto his arms Tracy had bought herself. The puzzles and games that littered the room, all virtually untouched except by the nurses, were the property of the hospital.

"Looks like we got everything," she informed Jake, walking him to the wheelchair. She gave the boy a reassuring smile. "It's going to be fine, Jake, I promise. Just you wait and see." Helping him onto the chair, she stepped back and looked at Adam. "Okay, Mr. Firefighter, looks like we're ready to roll."

Adam gave a short nod of his head. At first glance, there was no indication that he was anything but prepared for the venture that lay ahead. Only the deep breath he took before pushing the wheelchair out of the room gave him away.

And only to Tracy.

She smiled to herself as they went down the corridor to the elevator. It was nice to know that even superheroes had their human moments.

* * *

Stone tugged impatiently on the gunbelt resting at his hipline as he stood over Mitch Barnard. The latter was one of the three scientists who worked in the forensics laboratory of the crime investigation bureau. And the only one of the three Stone trusted to keep his mouth shut and erase any trail that might prove to be embarrassing to the police department, or specifically, to him.

He paced around the small, brightly lit room, stroking the pain in his gut. It felt like an ulcer. All he knew was that he hadn't had a decent night's sleep since this whole business began.

"Okay, so you're sure that none of the findings can be tied to Ingram?" They both knew that, if found, even fragments of the detonator cap could be traced.

The man sitting on the stool in the laboratory fingered the gold pin in his lapel, the one he'd been given for his outstanding service to the crime investigation department. The one Stone had personally given him. He was careful not to jab himself on the one sharp point the pin had. The area where the fourth leg was neatly severed off. It signified an even closer, more distinct circle than the real Lion's Den, for he, along with the twenty or so others who wore this particular version of the pin, were part of the chief's handpicked team.

And as such, he knew without being told where his allegiance lay.

Barnard gave Stone a smug look. He had been thorough. Nothing was going to leak out to point toward the actual culprit. Unless he wanted it to. "None whatsoever."

Stone knew better than to ask whether that meant there wasn't any actual damaging evidence found, or if whatever incriminating evidence did exist had been destroyed. Some topics were best left untouched.

"Good. We'll tell anyone who asks that the bombing is still an ongoing investigation, but that so far, it's not going very far." The chief smiled at his little play on words. He lay a hand on the other man's bony shoulder. "Nice work," he complimented Barnard before he left the room.

"Thanks," Barnard called after him.

Alone, he smiled to himself. The chief and Ingram owed him and he knew it. It was nice to be on the plus side of the column for a change. You never knew when you might need a favor. It was always good to have something to trade on, especially with a man like the chief, who wasn't exactly known far and wide for his evenhanded fairness. Quite the opposite was true.

Whistling, Barnard went back to his work.

Chapter 7

Unlocking the door to his garden apartment, Adam pushed it open and stepped out of the way, allowing Jake to go in first. The boy stood in the doorway for a moment, then took halting steps into the living room, as if each was being taken across a minefield and he was uncertain of his path.

"It's not much," Adam admitted.

His own needs were austerely simple. There were parts of his house that the fire hadn't reached. He'd salvaged what he could from them, mostly things that belonged to Bobby and Gloria, and moved into this small two-bedroom apartment to try to come to terms with the state his life was in. At no time was it about starting over, because he didn't want to start over. To start over meant to leave himself open to possibly feeling the gaping hole of deprivation all over again from a fresh point. He wasn't up to it.

"But you'll have your own room," he told the boy. Adam closed the door behind Tracy. "It's just down the hall, opposite mine."

The "hall" was all of three feet long, just off the living room.

The apartment was tiny. An echo would have trouble bouncing around, Tracy mused as she took in her surroundings. She'd taken a few hours off to look into Jake's background. A drive by the area showed her that the Andersons had lived in a sprawling, huge house with a pool and tennis courts visible out back. With no other next of kin to contest the will Daniel Anderson had left, the house belonged to Jake. But he needed a court appointed guardian and legal wheels turned slowly.

After living in such a big house this was going to take some getting used to for Jake, Tracy thought.

Adam placed a hand on the boy's shoulder as he guided him to the room that had been, until yesterday, his storage area. He'd cleaned the room out and then hastily bought a bed for Jake. Currently his belongings were distributed amid his siblings, tucked away in six different garages.

Jake winced from the contact. Adam immediately pulled back his hand, silently upbraiding himself for not being more careful. "Sorry."

Tracy quickly stepped in to alleviate the situation. "Healing's going faster than I anticipated," she told them both. "The two of you will be roughhousing in no time."

Adam didn't see that in the cards.

Considering the state of the rest of the house,

dishes in the sink, a shirt haphazardly tossed over the back of the sofa, several days' worth of newspapers scattered on the coffee table, Tracy was amazed at the pristine condition the second bedroom was in. There was a bed, a nightstand with a kid's baseball lamp and a bicycle parked beneath a window that looked out onto the communal pool.

From where she stood, she could see into Adam's room. The bed wasn't made and there was laundry strewn on the floor. The second bedroom had to have taken considerable effort on his part.

Jake took several steps into the room and went no farther. She gestured about the area. "What was this before today?"

A hint of a grin slowly worked its way to Adam's lips. The woman didn't miss much. "Storage area."

She was trying not to pay attention to the effect his grin was having on her pulse. The man's solemn expression didn't do him justice.

"What happened to the things?"

"My brothers and sisters let me use their garages for a while." Otherwise, even though the boy was small, there would have been no room for him amid all the other belongings. The room had held all the memories of his former life that he could safely deal with, things that had been important, in one way or another, to Gloria and Bobby. Things he couldn't get himself to part with. He just wished he'd been able to save more than a handful of photographs. But the fire had destroyed the albums that he and his wife had painstakingly put together.

She turned to Jake, trying to get him to come

around even a little. "A bed, a nightstand with a lamp and a bike. What more can a guy ask for, right, Jake?" Crossing to the last item, she ran her hand over the frame. Tracy noticed that the bicycle, a boy's model, had a slight dent in it and though in good condition, was not new. She looked at Adam. "Borrowed from a nephew?"

The bicycle had belonged to Bobby. His first two-wheeler. Adam could remember how excited his son had been when he'd first learned how to ride it.

Like a typical father, Adam had run behind it, holding on to the back of the seat until that all-crucial moment when he'd let go without telling Bobby. His son had made it a whole three yards before the boy had turned back to see if he was still holding on. The dent in the fender had come when Bobby had landed in the bushes, surprise throwing off his budding, wobbly coordination.

Bobby had brushed himself off and immediately gotten back up on the bike. He'd had that kind of spirit. Nothing daunted him. He was always eager to take on the world.

Adam felt a lump in his throat. "Yeah," he said shortly.

There was something more, Tracy thought. Something he wasn't saying. She looked into his eyes and saw the sorrow there. The same sorrow she saw in Jake's eyes. One thought fed into another. Could the bike have belonged to someone other than one of his nephews?

To a son, perhaps?

But Collins was obviously alone. He'd told her that

his wife had died. Could he have lost a child as well? Tracy knew she was making a huge leap here, but the loss of a son would go a long way toward explaining the bond that was knitting itself between the silent fireman and the mute little boy. Both had suffered losses. Jake was a fatherless child and Adam could very well be a childless father.

Two pieces of a whole that needed each other.

Adam saw the way Tracy was studying him, as if she were dissecting something. It made him feel uneasy. "What?"

She shook her head. Now was not the time to pry, or ask if she was guessing correctly. That wasn't why she'd come along. Her purpose was to help heal wounds, not open old ones. "Nothing, just wondering how the dent got there."

"Bushes," he told her matter-of-factly. "The bike crash-landed in the bushes."

With a novice riding it. His son? "Must have hurt."

Adam inclined his head in vague agreement. "He was a resilient kid."

Was.

The single word told her everything she needed to know. Sorry that she had touched upon such a raw nerve, she turned her attention back to Jake, her eyes smiling at the boy.

"Resilient. Just like you, right, Jake?"

For the first time, Jake looked at her when she said his name. Until now, if their eyes met at all, it was because she would place herself directly in his line of vision.

But that had been at the hospital. Here he was confronted with a different set of circumstances and he needed a way to relate, however peripherally.

Her stomach suddenly pinched, reminding her that she'd had only a slice of toast for breakfast. Tracy glanced at her watch.

"Okay, I'll tell you what," she announced, gently ushering Jake from the room. "Since it's coming on to noon, why don't I fix us all something to eat and then we can see about getting you settled in, making this place a little more your own, Jake."

Surprised, Adam followed her out to the kitchen. Jake trailed after them, stopping in the living room. "You're staying?"

Tracy turned around. He sounded surprised. "That was the plan."

He wasn't sure how he felt about this, about her staying in his apartment so long. Other than his sisters and sisters-in-law, no woman had stepped foot in here. This was his private territory.

"No one ran it by me."

It hadn't occurred to her that he wouldn't just take her presence for granted. "I'm sorry, I thought you understood I was coming along to help get Jake situated."

The word had a vague connotation. "I thought that meant just coming with him to the apartment."

She gave him a lopsided smile. "That's not situated, that's walking in. You get a lot more for your money with me." The smile turned into a tantalizing grin he had no idea how to read. "Now then, what would you like me to fix for lunch?"

She opened the refrigerator and then paused, her enthusiasm on momentary hold.

Aside from a lightbulb and shelves, there was a quarter of a loaf of white bread and what looked to be some leftover tuna fish salad in a bowl. The tuna fish had a sour odor to it. The bread, she was willing to bet, was probably turning a light green hue.

He'd been so busy clearing a place for the boy and turning down his siblings' offers to come help that Adam had forgotten all about stocking the refrigerator. The days he didn't eat at the station house, he ate out. Filling a refrigerator had never been a priority for him. He wasn't the kind to nibble. If he got the hungries at inopportune times, he just toughed it out.

Tracy closed the refrigerator again. Nothing to work with there.

"Well, seeing as how I'm not exactly up on my miracles and never got the hang of how to feed anyone using just a part of a loaf of bread and a bad fish salad, I'd say that one of us needs to make a run to the supermarket." She was vaguely aware that they had passed one on their way here, but how far away, she wasn't sure. "I'll give you first call."

He was at the door already, relieved for the break. "I'll go. What do you need?"

An instruction manual on what makes you tick. The thought snuck up on her from nowhere.

She was fairly certain she knew the way to the heart of a little boy. Or at least to his stomach. "Why don't you just pick up two pounds of ground beef— lean," she emphasized. "Ketchup, buns and pickles and I'll make some hamburgers for us. How's that?"

She looked at Jake for approval. After a beat, he nodded.

Another breakthrough, she mentally high-fived herself.

Though she didn't say anything about the boy's response, the sparkle in her eyes as she turned them on Adam gave her away.

It took him a second to gather up the thoughts that had scattered in response to the overwhelming exuberance he saw in her face. "Why don't I just go to a fast-food drive-through and save you the trouble?"

"No trouble." She liked to putter around in the kitchen and didn't get nearly enough time at it. "And this'll be healthier than what you can get there. We'll save the fast-food place for something special," she promised Jake. Her grin went up a degree, melting the tips of the laces on Adam's shoes. "Like maybe your first word."

"I won't be long," Adam promised, pulling the door open.

"Oh, and get some chicken. A cut-up fryer," she specified.

He looked at her. "To go with the hamburgers?"

"No, for dinner, silly."

That stopped him for a second. "You *are* spending the whole day."

She grinned. "Damn straight I am."

With what looked to be a resigned nod, Adam closed the door behind him.

She'd guessed right about coming here, she decided, turning away from the door. Good intentions notwithstanding, Adam wasn't quite comfortable with the boy yet.

"Okay, Jake," she said brightly. "Let's go set the table."

Though she'd expected him to be gone for a while, Adam was true to his word. He returned fairly quickly.

During Adam's absence, she'd kept up a steady stream of conversation with Jake while she explored Adam's kitchen. The firefighter had only the barest essentials available. One large pot, one small one and a single frying pan. Luckily, it was a large one. She was able to fry all three hamburgers at the same time. There was no need for anyone to wait for their serving.

Though he was slow to start, once he did, Jake ate with more appetite than she'd witnessed in the hospital.

Maybe he was feeling better, she thought happily. Being out of the hospital and taking small, baby steps into a brand-new life was having a positive effect on him.

She only hoped that it would continue.

With a surge of triumph, she caught Adam's eye and indicated Jake. When he got her meaning, they shared a smile.

Though he wasn't sure how he felt about it, Adam found that he had no say in the matter. Tracy spent the day.

After lunch, she drew both him and Jake into the

living room where she proceeded to locate specials on a station that featured live animal stories. Jake watched with mild interest, which Tracy clearly took to be another positive step. Adam had to admit that the programs didn't put him to sleep. That was something.

Afterward, there was a parade of different cartoon shows thanks to another channel, which was apparently where old cartoon programs went to die. Adam had grudgingly remained on the sofa after her silent entreaty, conveyed by her laying a hand on his knee and giving it a quick squeeze. He didn't know what amazed him more, her action or the fact that Tracy obviously took pleasure in such silly fare, apparently enjoying it every bit as much as any child.

What also surprised him was his reaction to her simple, intimate gesture. Having her touch his knee stirred him, reminding him of the kind of contact that had been missing from his life these past two years. The intimate shorthand between a man and a woman.

He sat beside Tracy, watching her as much as he watched the small screen. More.

The sound of her laughter echoed in his head, drifted through his system. Soft, melodious, like the promise of spring. It suited her.

And, in an odd way, it seemed to comfort him, though he wouldn't have been able to say why if anyone had asked him about it.

The day passed, remarkable only insofar as it came very close to approximating the family life he'd lost, with its days that defied recall, days that only left imprints of contentment in their wake.

It passed all too quickly.

After dinner, she'd had the boy help her pile the plates into the sink. That he did her bidding partially amazed Adam. But then, she was probably accustomed to getting men of all sizes to do what she wanted. She had that kind of a way about her, he decided. The kind of ability to make people want to do things for her.

He found himself wondering when his turn would come. What would she want of him?

The professional side of her emerged. Tracy took the boy into his room and changed his bandages just before bedtime. That done, she tucked him in and sat reading to him from books that mysteriously emerged from her bottomless bag, the same bag she'd brought the bandages in.

The woman was nothing short of amazing, Adam decided. She seemed prepared for everything, unruffled by anything.

She sat by the boy's bed, reading to him until he closed his eyes and finally drifted off to sleep. By then Adam had withdrawn to leave the two of them together. He figured she worked her magic better without an audience looking on.

As he waited for her to finish, Adam did something he rarely did. He was putting dishes away after having washed them. He'd just finished cleaning the roasting pan that Tracy had brazenly gone to the next-door neighbor and borrowed when she finally came out of Jake's room and walked into the kitchen.

"He's asleep," she announced with no small satisfaction.

"I kind of figured that."

Tossing the damp dishtowel aside, he looked at her. She looked tired, but happy. He found himself wondering why she wasn't married. Why wasn't she home somewhere, tucking her own kids into bed, reading them stories?

The questions surprised him. He didn't usually wonder about anyone. It wasn't like him. That was more the domain of the woman who lived across the way, Mrs. Wells, a widow who spent her entire day at the window, monitoring the comings and goings of everyone in the complex.

"You're really good with kids," he commented, walking into the living room with her.

She prided herself on that. "It's not hard. I really love them." For some reason, this touch of domesticity had left her with a bittersweet feeling. As if she was being given a glimpse of a life that would have been hers, if only things had turned out differently.

Tired, she sank down on the sofa for a moment. "That's the pity of it."

Without thinking, Adam sat down beside her. "Come again?"

She wasn't sure exactly what started her off. Maybe it was because he seemed interested. Or maybe she was just feeling vulnerable. Whatever the reason, she heard herself sharing with him what she hadn't told anyone but her best friend.

"I can't have any of my own. Ironic, isn't it?" A trace of a bitter smile played on her lips. "The lady pediatric doctor is barren." She shrugged. Talking about it didn't change anything. She had to accept it.

And she did. Over and over again, every single morning as the thought hurdled at her with the force of a comet entering the atmosphere when she first opened her eyes. "So I throw myself into my work to get my kid fix." She saw he wanted to ask, but respected privacy too much to invade hers. She liked that about him, his nobility. "I had a really bad bout of endometriosis."

The term was foreign to him. "I don't know what that is."

She laughed softly. "You're lucky. I do." Feeling suddenly cold, she wrapped her arms around herself and continued. "In a nutshell, it's a disease that messes with your reproductive system. Worse case, it destroys your ability to bear children." She remembered how devastated she'd felt when the doctor had first told her. She went into denial for over two months before she finally forced herself to accept the information. Her voice dropped to almost a whisper, as if she were talking only to herself. "I had worse case." Rousing herself, Tracy shook off the mood that was descending on her. "Things happen, I guess."

The urge to comfort her came from nowhere. Surprised, he banked it down. "Even to nice people."

She turned to look at him, her hand splayed over her heart. "My God, was that another compliment?"

He almost laughed at her comical exclamation. "An observation. You can do what you want with it."

"Is everyone in your family like you?" The voice that framed the question was teasing and kind. "You must have some pretty quiet Christmases if they are."

He liked setting her straight. "On the contrary, they can get pretty rowdy. Nobody notices if I don't talk."

She knew he was wrong there. "People always notice, they just might not say so." She could see that he was unconvinced. "I notice when you don't talk."

Now that he sincerely doubted. She liked the sound of her own voice too much. "It's hard getting a word in edgewise, even if I were so inclined."

"People have said that," she allowed with a grin that told him she wasn't insulted.

She was a good sport, he thought, who knew how to laugh at herself and only took herself seriously when the moment warranted it. The woman, he realized suddenly, had some pretty serious attributes. The fact that she couldn't bear children shouldn't have kept her from finding someone, Adam believed.

All in all, it had been a long day and her excuse for being in it was now asleep. Tracy rose to her feet. "So, I guess I'd better be going." Picking up her purse, she crossed to the door. Adam followed behind her. "I'll be by tomorrow around eight."

She kept managing to surprise him. He looked at her. "Tomorrow?"

"Yes." Impetuously, she'd spun the plan in the time it took her to walk from Jake's room to the kitchen. "I thought we'd go to an amusement park. Nothing fancy, just something to try to get a response from Jake. Ride the merry-go-round, eat cotton candy, that kind of stuff."

The week before the fire, he'd taken Bobby to an amusement park. He wasn't sure if he was up to this. "Don't you have to work?"

She wondered if it was an idle question, or if he was trying to not-so-subtly get rid of her. "I have a month's worth of a vacation. I decided to use a couple of days to get the two of you acclimated.''

She said "the two of you" rather than "the boy." The woman had a unique way of looking at things. "Think I need acclimating?"

Tracy believed in being honest whenever possible. "Yes, I do. From what I gather, you lead a very solitary life. Having him here is a culture shock to you as well as to Jake."

The ends of his mouth curved. "In a way, you're a culture shock. Should someone be acclimating me to you?"

She laughed, tickled. "I'd say you're doing just fine on your own."

Adam didn't know about that. But whether he was or not, there was no denying that she was going out of her way for him as well as the boy. He looked at her, his expression growing serious, as she placed her hand on the doorknob.

"Thanks for coming, Tracy."

Her eyes met his and she looked at him for a long moment.

"You know, that's the first time you've said my name." Her smile was wide. "I kind of like it."

As she had done the first time, Tracy rose up on her toes to brush her lips against his cheek.

He wasn't altogether sure what made him turn his head just then, but he did.

Their lips met in what appeared to be completely by accident.

Except that Adam knew better.

Chapter 8

Adam wasn't a man who ordinarily acted rashly. Common sense was his main hallmark.

Yet something impetuous had goaded him on at the very last second. If he'd stopped to think about it, he wouldn't have gone through with it.

But he didn't think, he reacted. Reacted to the scent of her perfume, to the sound of her laughter, which still hummed in his head like a distant melody. To the longing that had swept over him out of the shadows, reminding him that he was not a statue made of concrete and stone but a flesh and blood man.

And men had needs that sometimes took hold of them when they least expected it.

Tracy felt as if she'd been pierced by a flaming arrow.

Surprise faded in the face of heat that seared through her body like lightning traveling down a shiny metal rod. She felt Adam framing her face with his hands, felt herself leaning into the kiss, her perimeters swiftly melting into liquid, then mist.

He stole her breath away.

She didn't remember encircling his neck with her arms, didn't remember deepening the kiss that had begun as nothing more than a simple meeting of skin against skin.

Or had it?

Hadn't some deep, distant part of her secretly hoped for an accident such as this? Secretly wished that Adam Collins would react to her presence, would open himself up to her just the tiniest bit?

Maybe she had, but she'd never expected the results to be like this. It was like dipping her toes into the oncoming tide and suddenly finding herself swept away by a huge wave that engulfed her, body and soul, pulling her away from the shore and safety.

Safety. There wasn't any. Her skin tingled with excitement, with anticipation. Whatever this was, it definitely wasn't safe. She felt herself quivering. Longing.

Wanting him.

And then it was over.

Tracy wasn't sure who broke the connection, she only knew it was gone.

Blinking, she tested her lungs for air capacity before venturing a single word, unsure if she could even speak without her voice cracking.

One breath wasn't enough. She took another. She looked at him, still stunned. "Well, I didn't see that coming."

He'd overstepped the line, Adam upbraided himself. What the hell was the matter with him?

Sucking in air as subtly as possible, he ran a hand through his unruly hair. His expression was contrite, almost sheepish. There was no excuse.

"Sorry, I didn't mean—"

Before the sentence was out, she placed her fingers to his lips, silencing him. She didn't want him to spoil it. "I said I didn't see that coming. I didn't say I didn't like it."

He had no idea why he felt as if everything inside of him was smiling foolishly, like some schoolkid who'd stolen his first kiss.

He hadn't stolen, he'd taken, like a plundering Viking. Like some sex-starved animal. It was all he could do just to hold himself in check and pull away from her when all he'd wanted to do was continue. Continue and go on to the next level.

That wasn't like him.

He'd always been able to control what went on within him with little to no effort. Control was what he prided himself on. Control was all he had left. Except now he didn't.

She was being understanding and he appreciated it. "Still, I had no right to do that. This wasn't a way to repay you."

Unconsciously, she ran the tip of her tongue along her bottom lip. An aroused shiver coursed through her. "Maybe it was."

Adam didn't like this, didn't like his emotions tearing through the fabric of his resolve. Damn it, he *knew* better.

"It won't ever happen again," he promised her solemnly.

Oh God, she hoped that wasn't a prophesy. With effort, she kept her smile in place.

"The two words I've learned that don't count in this life are 'never' and 'forever,' both of which have the word 'ever' in them." There was a gentle kindness in her eyes as she looked up into his. "Let's just let things ride, okay?"

He started to protest, then thought better of it. Seeing who he was up against, it was probably useless to argue the point. The woman knew how to wield words better than anyone he'd ever met. Compared to her, he was an amateur.

So he heard himself saying, "Okay," even though he didn't mean it.

What he did mean was that it *wasn't* going to happen again, no matter what she said. He wasn't going to allow himself to be in that kind of a position again.

He couldn't. Because next time, he was afraid he might not be able to stop himself. Kissing her had unleashed something inside of him, something that was incredibly hungry. If he gave in to it, there was no telling where it would lead.

An awkward moment hung between them. Tracy pressed her lips together. She could still taste him. Her pulse began to race again.

"So, tomorrow?" she said again.

"Right. Tomorrow."

"See you," she murmured, leaving.

Adam slowly closed the door, telling himself he

had until tomorrow to pull himself together. A little more than twelve hours.

He didn't know if it was enough time.

It would have to be.

Like a myopic Cyclops, the red light on Tracy's answering machine was blinking at her madly, catching her eye the minute she walked into her apartment. There were three messages. Each one from Maureen. Each more urgent in its unabashed, mounting curiosity.

She debated calling the woman back, knowing she would wind up fielding questions and staying on the phone far longer than she really wanted to. She was tired and she intended to get an early start the next morning.

Petunia came trotting up to greet her. Squatting down, she petted the pig. "What do you think? Should I call Maureen back? She'll only talk my ear off and pump me for information."

The phone rang, taking the decision away from her.

"That's probably Maureen again," she told the attentive pig.

Besides, Maureen had gone out of her way for Jake, too, staying beyond her hours to keep the boy company when she was held up in surgery. The least she could do, Tracy decided, was satisfy the nurse's insatiable curiosity.

Blowing out a deep breath, Tracy picked up the receiver. "Hello."

"Finally. I was going to call the police and put out

an APB on you,'' Maureen declared in exasperation. ''Where have you been?''

Tracy took off her shoes and made herself comfortable on the sofa, tucking her legs under her. ''You know where I've been. With Jake.''

Tracy didn't have to be told that Maureen translated that to be, ''With Adam.'' The chuckle on the other end of the line was deep and appreciative, telling her she was right.

''All this time?''

Tracy told herself not to be resentful of Maureen's probing. She was just being cranky because she was tired, nothing else. ''He had trouble falling asleep.''

''Mr. Fireguy?''

''No,'' Tracy corrected tersely. Maureen knew damn well who she was talking about. ''Jake. I took the day off to be with the boy, remember?''

''I remember.'' There was a long, heartfelt sigh on the other end of the line. ''I'm just worried about your sex life, that's all.''

Tracy picked up the program guide from the coffee table and began to leaf through it, wondering if there was anything on television tonight she could fall asleep to. ''I don't have a sex life.''

''That's why I'm worried.'' Maureen sounded deeply frustrated. ''Didn't anything happen between the two of you?''

Tracy tossed the guide aside. ''Jake responded to something I said.''

''That's great.'' Maureen dismissed the information. Right now, she was after something more stimulating. ''But I mean the *other* two of you.''

Tracy didn't believe in carrying teasing too far. She decided to throw her best friend a small morsel. "He kissed me."

"He what?" There was excitement in Maureen's voice, but the next moment, it was siphoned off as caution entered. "Wait a second, we're talking about Mr. Fireguy, right? Not the boy."

Tracy smiled despite herself as the scene came flooding back to her. "We're talking about Mr. Fireguy."

"Tell me," Maureen begged. "Tell me *everything*."

Maureen would have her dissecting every pause, every breath if she let her. Tracy knew she wasn't up to that tonight. She began to scratch Petunia behind the ears. "There's nothing to tell. I was leaving, he said thank you and I kissed his cheek."

Maureen's disappointment was palatable. "I thought you said—"

Her generous nature made her cave in. "And then he turned his head and suddenly, it wasn't his cheek I was kissing anymore. It was him."

She could almost see Maureen's eyes light up. "And he kissed back." It wasn't so much a question as a vicarious excursion.

"Yes." The sigh, dreamy rather than exasperated, escaped before Tracy could think to stop it. "He kissed me back."

"How was it?"

Though she shared pretty much everything with the other woman, there were some things that remained more special if they weren't dragged out into the light of day. Or over the phone lines.

"Maureen—"

"C'mon, Trace," Maureen begged, "Throw me a bone here." She threw in the kicker to tip the scales in her favor. Tracy was nothing if not scrupulously fair. "I've just put together a box of clothes for Jake and I've thrown in some of Isaac's old storybooks and toys. The least you can do is give me something to fantasize about."

"That's bribery."

"Well, sure." She said it as if she was surprised it might be viewed as anything else. "Never said that it wasn't." Tracy laughed in response. "So give, how was it?"

Oh what the hell, why not? It wasn't as if she had some kind of a relationship with the man. For all she knew, he was right, this was a one-time fluke. "I'm surprised I'm still wearing shoes."

Eager to get the full impact, Maureen wasn't sure she understood. "As in knocking them off your feet?"

"As in burning them off my feet."

Maureen squealed with satisfaction. "I knew it, I knew it. The first second I saw those lips of his, I knew he was a great kisser."

Petunia was getting restless. Lodging the telephone receiver between her shoulder and neck, Tracy used both hands to pull the small animal onto the sofa. The pig curled up against her, waiting to be petted.

"Well, you knew more than me," Tracy told the other woman.

"Yeah, right." Like she believed that. She'd seen the way Tracy had looked at the man when she'd thought no one else was looking. There was definite interest there. "You really should get out more, Tracy. So then what happened?" Maureen pressed eagerly again.

Time to wrap this up. "And then I left," Tracy told her matter-of-factly.

"Wait a second. He practically incinerates you and you just walk away? Forgive me, Tracy, but I'm not buying this."

"Slowly," Tracy told her. "I walked away slowly." What was the harm in admitting it? "My knees felt kind of wobbly."

There was a prolonged sigh on the other end. Tracy wondered if Maureen's husband was overhearing any of this. "So why didn't you stay? Maybe indulge a little in sheet music?"

Maybe it was because she was tired, but Maureen had lost her. "Sheet music?"

Maureen wondered if her friend was deliberately playing dumb. "Warming the sheets, knocking boots—you know."

"What I know, Maureen, is that you have one hell of an incredible imagination. It's a long way between being kissed by a man and sleeping with him."

Maureen's laugh was deep and throaty, and full of innuendoes. "Who said anything about sleeping? So, what's next on the agenda?"

"I go to bed—alone." That wasn't strictly true, she thought, looking at Petunia. "I'm beat."

"I mean with Mr. Fireguy. When are you seeing him again?"

The pig put her head in Tracy's lap. Tracy began to feel guiltier about neglecting the animal. *Soon,* she mouthed to the pet. "We're taking Jake to the amusement park tomorrow."

"Good, good. You're spending the whole day together, right?"

It was time to stop indulging Maureen's fantasies and set her straight. "I think you're losing focus here, Maureen. This is about the boy."

"Of course it is," Maureen agreed. "But there's no reason why it can't be about the man, too." Knowing how Tracy's mind worked, she appealed to her softer side, the side that had a tendency to mother everyone. "I saw the look in his eyes. That man needs somebody."

As Tracy saw it, that was why he had bonded with the boy. "Well, he has somebody. Jake."

"Somebody taller," Maureen insisted. "You might as well face it, Trace, I'm not going to let up until you have a significant other in your life."

She smiled as Petunia snuggled further against her lap. Leaning over, she scratched the pig behind the ear. "I have a significant other. Petunia."

Maureen huffed in her ear, clearly at the end of her patience. "I was talking about something that can't be turned into a side of pork."

Pretending that Petunia could understand every word, Tracy covered the mouthpiece. "She didn't mean it," she told the pig.

"God." Maureen groaned loudly. "This man has

come into your life just in time, girl. You're talking to pigs now.''

Petunia was the last in a long line of pets and Tracy had spoken to every one as if they had a healthy command of the English language and a decent attention span. There was something soothing and private about bonding with a pet.

''I'll have you know that I talk to Petunia all the time.''

Maureen surrendered some ground, knowing this was getting her nowhere. ''Beats talking to yourself, I guess. But, like I said, this man has come into your life just in time.''

''Adam Collins is only in my life insofar as we are both interested in helping Jake.''

The assertion didn't daunt Maureen's enthusiasm. There were high hopes at work here. ''Everyone needs a common starting point,'' she allowed magnanimously. Maureen knew when to retreat. She'd gained enough information for one night and didn't want to jeopardize further communication. ''So when do you want me to drop by with the box of things?''

If Maureen came over to her house, it would probably take dynamite to dislodge her and Tracy *was* tired. She just had enough energy left to feed Petunia and take the pig out for a short walk.

Maybe that kiss *had* drained her, she thought.

''Tell you what, why don't I swing by your place tomorrow morning before I drive over to Adam's apartment.''

''Fine.'' Maureen was clearly disappointed. Tracy could hear it in her voice. ''I'm on duty at nine.''

Perfect. She knew it took Maureen half an hour to get to the hospital. "I'll be there at eight-thirty."

"You don't play fair," Maureen pouted.

"Never claimed I did. See you tomorrow."

She heard Maureen grumble something on the other end. With a laugh, Tracy hung up the phone, then slipped it back on the side table beside the answering machine.

Petunia sat looking up at her patiently, almost as if she understood that something different had happened tonight.

Tracy smiled at the animal. "No hiding things from you, is there, girl?" She chucked Petunia under her small chin. "You know, you're as intuitive as a dog."

Rising from the sofa, she placed the pig carefully on the floor and then went to look for Petunia's leash. It had a habit of traveling during the day and Tracy strongly suspected the pig liked whipping it around.

She found it tucked under the kitchen table.

Tracy crossed back into the living room, kneeling down beside the pig.

"I don't mind telling you, because I know you won't let this go any further, but part of me kind of wished Collins'd kept on kissing me and maybe even—well, you know." Incredible though it was, she felt a blush creeping up her cheek when she thought of the two of them making love together. "I don't have to explain the birds and the bees to you, do I?"

Petunia looked up at her with soft brown eyes as she hooked the leash onto her collar.

"Maybe I do at that. Haven't seen many boyfriends coming by, ringing the bell for you, either." On her feet again, Tracy checked her pockets for her house keys before going to the front door. "Maybe I'll ask him if he has a friend for you next time."

Tracy shook her head and laughed to herself. "Maybe Maureen is right. I don't get out enough. And neither do you."

Maybe that explained it. Explained why she'd been so bowled over when Adam had kissed her. The last time she'd been kissed, someone had planted a quick one on her lips the December before last because she'd inadvertently walked under a sprig of mistletoe while writing notes into a patient's folder. Dr. O'Malley had smelled of hot chili peppers thanks to the dip one of the nurses had brought. It had been enough to make a person contemplate everlasting celibacy.

She *did* need to get out more.

As Tracy opened the door, an idea came to her. Petunia might be just what the doctor ordered. She was gentle, sweet-tempered and infinitely adorable.

"Tell you what, I can't do it tomorrow, but I'm off the next day, too. Why don't I take you with me then and you can meet Adam yourself? Tell me what you think. If nothing else, I know Jake'd love to meet you." She bit her lower lip. "At least, I hope so. I need a way to get to him, to make him talk. Maybe I'll show him how we play hide and seek." Infinitely trainable, the pig had learned how to track her if she kept Petunia's favorite food, truffles, in her pocket.

Tracy began to walk out. "You know, you're really easy to talk to, Petunia, but I wish you had a few more opinions of your own."

The pig squealed slightly, as if in response. "You're right. We've got a good thing going here. I talk, you listen. Why mess it up?"

Tracy took the pig's silence as an agreement.

Chapter 9

Afetr giving it some thought, Adam decided to ignore it.

Ignore the kiss, ignore what had prompted it and the avalanche of feelings that had quickly risen up in its wake. Feelings he wasn't up to dealing with.

It was simpler this way and a lot less uncomfortable if he just pretended that the kiss had never happened. Otherwise, it and what it had consequently generated would be there between them, making things awkward for them. For him.

For the duration that he and Tracy had to interact, he wanted to keep things moving smoothly.

Besides, other than today and tomorrow, he reasoned in the wee hours of the night, the extent of their interaction might be exchanging a few words as he came in or went out while she was there to stay with Jake. Since he'd been inundated with offers of help by a family that was relieved to see him finally functioning among the living, he might take Tina or one of the others up on their offers to stay with Jake while he worked. That would do away with the need for Tracy altogether.

The need for Tracy.

The words shimmered in his head, teasing him. He had a need all right, and he wasn't happy about it.

All this was temporary, anyway, he told himself as he lay in bed, watching the shadows of passing cars chase one another along his ceiling. Certainly there was nothing permanent in the offing. Jake would be gone soon and with him, Tracy.

There was no need to give the incident any more weight than it deserved. He'd acted like a man, reacted to outside stimulus. After all, the woman was far from ugly.

Very far from ugly.

As a matter of fact, he felt that the term "dropdead gorgeous" might have been coined with someone like her in mind.

He punched his pillow, trying to find a place for himself. Failing.

Didn't matter.

All this would be behind him in a little while. And all that actually did matter was the boy, not some dormant hormones that had chosen the wrong time to wake up.

Silence on the subject was the best route, Adam insisted. A woman like Dr. Tracy Walker was probably kissed a great deal on a regular basis, as well as wined and dined often. In all likelihood, she'd probably forgotten all about it.

Unlike him.

But that was because all of his thoughts were centered around this latest upheaval in his life and unfortunately all things that concerned the boy brought the woman to mind as well.

He was going to have to work on that.

Starting now.

It was a promise he made to himself several times during the night, each and every time he woke up, which was frequently.

He was a light sleeper. Being on alert at the fire station had done that to him. So now, with this new person he was responsible for sleeping in a room only a few feet away from his, and a woman he had no business thinking about preying wantonly on his mind, he wasn't exactly the perfect candidate for a good night's sleep. Or much rest at all.

He should have never kissed her, Adam upbraided himself more than once during the course of the restless night.

And maybe he shouldn't have volunteered so quickly to be there for the boy, either. The thought snuck in somewhere before dawn. After all, there was family services waiting to take over. The people in that department were far better suited to dealing with this situation. And, on top of that, he'd discovered that there was a family lawyer out there somewhere overseeing the Andersons' estate. He could find some kind of guardian for the boy.

Trouble was, the lawyer was out of the country on vacation.

Everyone who had any connection to the boy seemed to be out of the country, Adam had thought angrily. Except for him.

And Tracy.

Unable to sleep, Adam got out of bed a total of four times to check on Jake. Moving as quietly as he could, Adam eased open the door to the boy's room and peered in. Each time, he saw that the boy was asleep.

And each time he looked at Jake, Adam felt guilty for thinking about pushing the "problem" on to someone else. Jake wasn't a "problem," he was a little boy who had gone through a traumatic experience. He had no business thinking about deserting him, because that was what it was, pure and simple. Desertion.

It was the woman who had scrambled his thinking process, Adam thought as he wearily made his way back to bed a fourth time. And he had let her.

Well, no more.

The self-issued warning was hovering somewhere in his hazy brain when Adam heard a ringing noise. More exhausted now than he had been when he'd first gone to bed, it took him a second to come to and identify the source of the sound.

The second ring had him sitting bolt upright in bed, thinking emergency.

That faded as orientation set in. He wasn't at the fire station, he was home. Home, but not alone. It wasn't an alarm, the ringing he heard was a doorbell. His doorbell.

Muttering under his breath, Adam reached for the jeans he'd discarded the previous evening and pulled them on over the briefs he slept in. As an afterthought, he tossed off the football jersey he'd worn last night and picked up an undershirt from the floor he mistook for a shirt as he made his way to the front door.

Clouds of sleep were just beginning to evaporate from his brain and his vision was attempting to focus as he pulled open the door.

"Yeah?"

The greeting on Tracy's lips disappeared the moment her eyes swept over the man in the doorway who was sleepily leaning against the front door. Her throat went dry.

He was bare-chested, with snug denim jeans hanging off his lean hips. The top button on his jeans had been left undone. There were wall-to-wall muscles residing beneath a smooth, hard chest and above a waist that was taut and flat enough to lick a serving of ice cream off of.

It took Tracy a second to work up enough moisture in her mouth to reform the word she'd originally intended to say.

"Hi."

Even though it took effort as she pushed it up along an incredibly parched throat. The word was breathless, as if she'd run up two flights of stairs at breakneck speed to deliver it.

She looked like sunshine in a fringed, brown

leather jacket. She had on jeans that appeared to have been painted on and black boots that looked as if they'd long since been broken in. Sleepy though he was, he could appreciate what he saw. Adam struggled not to allow fantasy to take over.

One last yawn broke its way out. "What are you doing here?"

"Do the words 'amusement park' ring a bell?" she asked, searching his face for some kind of sign that a light was going on in his head.

Damn, but a man shouldn't look this good getting out of bed, where he had obviously been a few seconds before she'd arrived. The state of his mussed-up hair, his almost unfocused eyes and the light stubble on his chiseled face told her that he'd been warming his sheets as she'd been pulling into the parking spot.

Warming the sheets.

Maureen's term.

Tracy tried not to think about the rest of what Maureen had said last night, but it wasn't easy, given the state the man before her was in. It reminded her that it had been a very long time since a man had touched her as if she were anything other than a physician who was there to perform miracles on call.

Wow, was all she could think. Why hadn't someone snatched up this man? What sort of baggage was he carrying around that would ward women away from him?

"Amusement park," Adam repeated, mumbling the words as he waited for them to make some kind of sense to him. She'd mentioned something about that last night, right? "That was today."

She didn't know if he was asking her a question, or just saying the words to have them register in his head. In either case, Tracy provided reinforcement. "That was today."

Stretching taut, stiff muscles, he looked at his watch, trying to make out the numbers. What time was it anyway? "But not at dawn."

"It's not dawn," she informed him cheerfully. "It's almost nine. Half the day is gone."

He snorted in disdain. "For who? The people in Australia?"

"You need coffee," she told him. Maybe a whole gallon of it, she added silently as she bent over to pick up the box at her feet. A rather large, unwieldy cardboard box.

"I need sleep," he countered. "Give me that," Adam ordered. He didn't wait for her to comply but took the box out of her hands. It wasn't heavy, but its size made it bulky and awkward. Just the way he felt around her right now. "What is this, anyway?"

"Clothes from one of the nurses." She led the way back into his apartment. It didn't get the morning sun, she noticed, looking at the darkened living room. "She has a son a little older than Jake and he's outgrown a lot of his clothes. I thought these might come in handy," she placed a hand flat against the box he was carrying, "until we can get some of his own for him—whenever his lawyer gets back."

He didn't have a lawyer, it felt strange to think of

Jake as having one of his own. Adam deposited the box on the coffee table.

"Did you know that there's a woman in the apartment across from yours who sits at her window, watching every move I make?"

He nodded. "Mrs. Wells. She watches every move everyone makes. It's her hobby."

Tracy looked over her shoulder, although there was now a door in her way, obscuring her line of vision. "Poor thing, doesn't she have any friends?"

Even sleepy, he could tell where this was going. "Why don't you just concentrate on Jake for the time being, all right?"

"All right," Tracy agreed, though she made a mental note to wave at the woman the next time she saw her, perhaps even strike up a conversation if the woman opened her window.

Adam didn't think he won his point so easily, but he wasn't about to press the point and question her. "Good idea," he mumbled.

"I have another one." He turned to look at her, the wary look in his eyes telling her that he was bracing himself. The man had a long way to go before he became trusting, she thought. "Breakfast." She held up the plastic supermarket bag that had been looped on her arm as she'd walked in. "I stopped at the market and picked up bread, eggs and orange juice. Milk for Jake. And I saw you didn't have any coffee, so I brought instant." She hadn't noticed any coffee machine visible. "We'll have your refrigerator looking like a normal one in no time," she promised. "Jake up yet?"

"No," he said, following her into the kitchen. He didn't like the way she was barging into his life, re-arranging it on him. He scowled at her, picking apart what she'd said. "Aren't eggs bad for you?"

"Not really," she assured him. She began opening cupboards, looking for the frying pan she'd used yesterday. "They've been much maligned. In moderation, eggs are good for you." Success arrived in the third cupboard. She took out the frying pan, placing it on the stove's burner. "That's the key, moderation." She looked at him an enigmatic smile on her lips. "But I guess I don't have to tell you that."

Was that some sort of snide comment at his expense? "What's that supposed to mean?"

She lined up six eggs one after another along the counter. "That you don't strike me as someone who just jumps right into a situation without carefully examining and evaluating it." She looked up at him for a second. "That's what makes what you did so special."

She was talking about him kissing her, Adam thought, bracing himself.

Well, maybe it was better out in the open. They'd talk about it, he'd deal with it, push it aside and forget about it.

Just as soon as the erotic dreams about her faded.

The thought descended on him like thunder. Until this moment, he hadn't remembered that he'd had erotic dreams last night.

He felt a fresh rush of discomfort assault him. "Look, about that—"

She seemed not to hear him. "It isn't every man who'd take in a child."

Adam was brought up short and he stopped dead in his tracks. She wasn't talking about what had happened between them, she was talking about Jake.

Chagrined, embarrassed at his narcissistic thoughts, Adam blew out a breath as he dragged a hand through his unruly hair. "Yeah, well, I don't know if that's such a great idea."

Her eyes narrowed as she tried to process what had just been said between them. Was he backing out? Had something happened last night after she'd left to make him change his mind?

"What do you mean?"

He shrugged. It wasn't anything he hadn't already shared with her. It had just loomed a little larger, a little darker, during his almost-sleepless night.

"I'm a stranger to him. Maybe Jake'd be better off in his own house, with some kindly neighbor staying with him, or—"

She wasn't going to let him build up a full head of steam. The locomotive wasn't about to be allowed to leave the station. "You're the best thing for him."

He wished he could believe that. It would make things easier. "What makes you think so?"

"The way he looks at you. Like it or not, he's made you his new father figure."

The thought brought a cold chill down his spine. He wasn't a father figure. He wasn't even a father anymore. If he'd been a decent one, then maybe Bobby would still be alive.

"Hey, I'm not—"

"Yes, you are," Tracy said firmly, kindly, cutting through any protest he might have been about to make. "To him."

She bit her lip. Jake could walk in on them at any moment and she didn't want this to be the topic of conversation the boy overheard. He might misunderstand and think he wasn't wanted. That wasn't what he needed to hear at the moment.

"How do you like your eggs?" she asked cheerfully as if the other topic had never been voiced.

"In the carton." Adam wasn't hungry, he was in turmoil. About a lot of things. "I haven't eaten eggs in years."

As always, she put only a positive spin on what he said. "So you won't be bored with them." Not to be dissuaded, she tried again. "When you did eat eggs, how did you have them prepared?"

The woman was incorrigible. And the prettiest pit bull he had ever seen. "Sunny-side up. That's—"

"I know what sunny-side up means," she told him, already beginning to crack eggs against the side of the frying pan. "That's the way I like them, too." She nodded toward the back. "Why don't you go and wake Jake up while I get this going?"

He decided that the minor errand would be safer than standing here, half-dressed, looking at her and entertaining thoughts that were light-years away from breakfast, amusement parks or orphaned little boys.

But as he turned to go to Jake's room, he abruptly stopped.

"No need," he told her. "Jake's already up."

Tossing another empty shell aside, she looked over

her shoulder. Her eyes smiled just as warmly as her lips as she looked at the boy standing in the doorway. He'd dressed himself, putting on the same clothes he'd worn yesterday. His shirt was misaligned.

"Hi, Jake. Did I wake you?"

He shook his head, walking into the room. Tracy spared Adam a glance before looking back at the boy. He might not be talking, but he was responding. Part of the wall that existed between him and the world was slowly coming down.

"I'm making eggs for breakfast." The last egg dropped out of the shell she'd cracked. Tracy tossed the shell away. "I took a guess that you might like them sunny-side up. That's the way Adam takes them and I figured all he-men liked their eggs that way."

"If that's the case, what's your excuse?" Adam asked, nodding at the third set of eggs she had frying.

She cocked her head comically, winking at Jake. "I'm a she-man?"

Almost against his will, Adam's eyes swept over her again. Tracy had shed her jacket. She was wearing a light green, long-sleeved sweater that brought out the green in her eyes and accented her chest, making him acutely aware of the difference between men and women.

It also made his palms itch.

"Not hardly," he muttered under his breath.

The quick grin on her face told him she'd heard him. It went straight to his gut. He needed to put some space between them. Preferably a lot, but he'd settle for the bedroom right now.

"I'd better go and put some clothes on," he told her, already backing out.

It was hard for her to look at his eyes, not while the rest of him was so temptingly delicious. But she made the effort and was successful.

"Good idea." Her mouth curved in some secret joke he wanted to share. "You might get cold on the rides, dressed like that."

That brought another thing to mind, something he hadn't raised last night when she'd come up with this idea. "Speaking of cold, don't you think it's too cold for a day at the amusement park?"

"It's not too cold," she contradicted. "It's invigorating, bracing. I used to go ice skating in weather that was much colder than this. Besides, think of the upside. There'll be less people to contend with." She looked at Jake to see if he was listening. His eyes were on her. She found that vastly encouraging. "More rides per hour."

He might have known she'd say something like that. In little more than two weeks in her company, he was swiftly beginning to be able to read her. Still, he felt compelled to ask, "Are you always this nauseatingly optimistic?"

She ran the edge of the spatula along the rim of the eggs, making sure they weren't sticking. "In varying degrees, yes. Never saw the advantage in seeing the dark side."

He laughed shortly. "It's less disappointing that way."

"No," she contradicted, "it starts out disappointing that way. My way there's at least hope for a little while.''

He sighed. There was no arguing with the woman. He didn't even know why he'd attempted to bother. ''I'll go get dressed.''

She nodded, trying not to watch Adam as he left the room.

There was no denying that he had a butt that was almost heart-stopping. The man looked damn good, coming and going. She sighed, getting her mind back on what she was doing.

Reinforcing her smile, Tracy looked down at the boy standing beside her.

''I'm glad you're up, Jake. I need someone to help me with the toast.'' She glanced over toward the toaster that resided forlornly on the counter and prayed that it hadn't rusted from disuse. Adam made it sound as if he never ate at home and from the looks of his refrigerator, she had no reason to doubt him. ''Just open up the loaf of bread over there and drop two slices in for me, would you?''

She held her breath as she pretended to watch the frying eggs. After a prolonged moment, Jake reached for the loaf of bread on the counter.

Yes! Tracy thought, mentally fisting her hand and bringing her elbow down to her side in triumph.

Chapter 10

She could feel his eyes on her. Adam'd been looking at her for most of the trip back from the amusement park. He'd said very little, but she'd come to expect that from him.

But she hadn't expected the scrutiny, if that was what it actually was. They'd spent the entire day together, she and Adam and Jake. Was there something on his mind he was searching for a way to phrase?

Or was Adam just absentmindedly staring off into space and she just happened to be in his direct line of vision?

Tracy turned down a less-traveled street, her eyes on the road.

She sighed. Well, if Mohammed wasn't coming to the mountain, the mountain damn well was going to have to come to him. She kept her face forward.

"You know, you've been staring at me for most of

the drive home. What's the matter, do I have a smudge on my cheek or something?''

''No.'' Adam shifted uncomfortably in his seat. He hadn't realized he was being that obvious.

They were on their way home after putting in what he deemed to be *more* than a full day at the amusement park. Tracy had elected to take her truck and he hadn't seen the need to object. The truck had surprised him. She didn't seem the type to drive a vehicle like this. She'd seemed more at home behind the wheel of her other car, the sporty Mustang—until he saw her climb into the cab of the truck.

The woman looked at home no matter where she was.

Jake was dozing between them. The boy still hadn't said a single word, but there was no denying that he'd had a good day. Once or twice, Adam was certain that he saw a smile trying to emerge, trying to mirror what was most definitely in the boy's eyes.

Now that was a coincidence. Jake smiled with his eyes, just like Tracy.

Except that Tracy was more like a damn beacon, Adam thought, dispensing sunlight from her eyes. Hell, from every part of her. He had a feeling that if she put her mind to it and stretched out her hands, she could probably shoot sunbeams from her fingertips.

He shook his head, the notion taking him by surprise. Shooting sunbeams from her fingertips? Just how dumb was that? It seemed to him as if he had very little control over his mind these days.

Was it because of the boy, because he'd taken on this extra load in his life?

Or was it because of the woman?

Seemed like nothing was the same since he'd rushed into that burning building at the Lone Star Country Club.

He realized that she was still waiting for an answer. "I was just wondering where you get all your energy from, that's all."

She hadn't thought of herself as being extraordinarily energetic today. This was a typical day for her. Tracy shrugged. "Never gave it much thought."

Well, he had. Watching her all day, not just keeping up with Jake but more often than not, leading the way. And dragging him in her wake, goading him on to stay abreast of her and the boy. He'd thought about it a lot. About her energy.

About her.

Adam cleared his throat, then smiled. Sort of. "You might try giving some thought to finding a way to bottle that. Could make a mint if you did. Hell, woman, you've got more energy than anyone else I've ever encountered."

"Just business as usual," she told him. Tracy spared a glance at the boy who sat between them in the truck, his head nodding to the side as he slept. "I just wanted him to have a good time." She raised her eyes to Adam's. "Think he had a good time?"

"Yeah, I do."

She nodded, not wanting to probe any further, content with the knowledge that she'd helped bring a little diversion and pleasure into the boy's life.

The contentment needed a mate.

Tracy glanced at Adam again when she came to a red light, easing her foot slowly down on the brake. "How about you?"

The question interrupted his thoughts. About her. "How about me what?"

She smiled. The man definitely had a short attention span. "Did you have a good time?"

He examined the physical evidence. The temperature had never risen above forty degrees, although the sun had made it seem warmer at times. At least it hadn't snowed, he thought. "My lungs are cold, my feet hurt and I think my fingers are frozen and might just break off."

Her mouth curved broadly. She was getting used to sifting out the complaints from the actual emotion he was trying to bury beneath it. "I didn't ask for an inventory, Collins, I asked you if you had a good time."

He blew out a breath, leaning back in his seat, his arm protectively around the boy's shoulders. "Yeah, I guess I did, at that."

"Good." A straight answer. "My work here is done," she murmured with a laugh.

Her soft voice sent ripples out into the velvety darkness that existed within the cab of the truck. Warming him. Igniting feelings. He blanketed them, stamping them out as best he could, the way he would a single flame that might lead to a fire.

"So should I be on my guard tomorrow?" he heard himself asking to dispel the sultry silence that was swaddling around him.

The man was still an enigma to her. "What do you mean?"

"Should I be up at dawn, waiting for you to descend?" She'd said something about having another day off. So did he.

Tracy laughed, shaking her head. He sure had a way with words. "You make me sound like a Mongolian horde, about to loot and plunder."

"Maybe not a Mongolian horde exactly, and maybe not looting…"

At a light, she turned to look at him. "But plundering?" It took her a second to realize that he was pulling her leg.

"Plundering my energy."

Tracy laughed softly. She had a hunch that under the right circumstances, Adam Collins had plenty of energy to spare. But for the sake of the way the conversation was going, she merely said, "Maybe you don't eat right, Collins." He didn't if that refrigerator of his was any indication. "Although you were keeping up just fine today."

Maybe he was tired. That was why his guard was down. Whatever the reason, he admitted, "That was just my male pride."

She arched a brow, amused. "Can't be outdone by a woman?"

His expression was unreadable. "Something like that."

She slanted a look at him as she took a right turn. "Funny, you don't seem the type to be bothered by something that trivial."

She had a lot to learn about the male ego, Adam

thought. It occurred to him that he wouldn't mind teaching her. "It's only trivial if you're on the winning side."

"I had no idea this was a competition."

There it went, that same sunlight in her eyes, he noted. As if she had some kind of secret joke she was teasing him with before she shared it.

Damn but he wanted to share those secrets with her. Wanted her.

"If I'd known," she was saying, "I would have tried harder."

He merely groaned, hoping that it would hide what he was really thinking and feeling.

"Looks like we're here," she announced.

He looked and saw his apartment complex on the right. He'd had no idea they were so close. It wasn't like him to be this disoriented.

Guiding the vehicle into the first available spot in the guest parking lot, Tracy pulled in and then put on the emergency brake. For a second, she debated just having Adam take Jake out of the truck and then leaving, but she realized that she wasn't quite ready to see the evening end just yet.

She shut off the engine and got out on her side of the truck. Rounding the rear of the vehicle, she came to Adam's side just as he was slowly drawing Jake out, taking extra care not to wake or disturb him too much.

It felt as if he was doing this in slow motion. "I'm really afraid of hurting him," he confessed.

She liked that about him, liked his sensitivity to someone else's pain, especially someone so young.

"He's healing at a remarkable rate. The pain dissipates long before the visible signs are gone," she assured him. The therapist, Randi, was scheduled to come tomorrow to work with Jake. After seeing how he got around today, Tracy doubted too many visits were going to be necessary.

Then, because she had a natural tendency both to take charge and to be nurturing, Tracy said, "Here, let me help."

Not waiting for him to say anything, she wiggled in in front of Adam in order to pick Jake up.

The contact should have been muted by the layers of clothing that existed between them. But somehow, the jackets, both sheepskin and leather, didn't take the edge off the jolt of electricity that flashed through Adam as Tracy's body brushed up against his.

There'd been no one in his life since he'd lost his wife, not even a casual one-night stand. Adam told himself that was the reason behind what he was feeling. All this was just a physical reaction to a beautiful woman.

But even so, it was getting harder and harder to deny, harder to control.

Adam stepped back from her as if he'd touched a live wire. Had he felt it, too? she wondered. That wild bolt of lightning that had seared through her. Because right now, the man was making her absolutely rethink her celibate position. And the scales were tipped his way.

She'd always felt that casual couplings were not for her. That when she slept with someone it would be because she felt she was with the right man, a man she wanted to marry and have a family with. Since having a family was no longer part of the equation, no longer possible, she'd abandoned the rest of it, too. The kind of man she would give her heart to *wanted* children, children she wouldn't be able to give him.

Now she wasn't so sure about her stand. If she was any judge of people, Collins was most definitely not in the market for a lifelong partner. He wasn't looking to get married any time soon. Probably never.

Yet more and more, he was occupying a place in her thoughts. She would have been more than happy to attribute that to Maureen and her far-from-subtle hints about her making love with the tall, dark and oh-so-handsome fireman.

But the truth of it was she couldn't pin the blame on Maureen, couldn't pin it on anyone but herself. She wanted it, wanted to make love with Adam.

What remained to be seen now was if she was going to go through with it.

Tracy smiled to herself as she handed the boy off to Adam. She was making it sound as if this was a foregone conclusion, as if the man's wishes were something she was already privy to. Maybe Adam *didn't* want to make love with her.

She raised her eyes to his.

Yeah, she thought, he did.

An old, absurd song title from the twenties crossed her mind. "Your Lips Tell Me No, No, But There's Yes, Yes In Your Eyes." There was most definitely "yes, yes," in Adam's eyes.

And it thrilled her beyond words.

Tracy looked down at the boy the firefighter was

holding. Such wanton thoughts arising out of what was actually such an altruistic scenario. Damn, but she was getting to be bad.

Adam had no idea what was going on in her head, only that Tracy was looking at him strangely. Maybe she'd felt it, too, he mused. Felt that pull that had flashed between them. Trouble was, he didn't know what he wanted to do about it.

Liar.

A small, knowing inner voice mocked him. He did know, he knew exactly what he wanted to do about it. But he wasn't going to, Adam told himself.

Making love with this woman would only complicate his life even more. Hopelessly so. Not that she would make waves, he was almost positive that she wouldn't. She seemed too free-spirited to think that a man pledged his heart after sharing one torrid night with a woman. But if he made love with her, he wasn't sure if he could keep his emotions out of it. And once they were brought forth, who the hell knew what would happen?

Better not to start than to deal with what came in the aftermath.

"I'm inviting myself over for coffee," she informed him as, much to his surprise, she began to lead the way to his apartment. "And you can't tell me you don't have any because I brought it this morning."

This wasn't retreating, this was riding straight into the fray. Not a good idea. Adam said the first thing that occurred to him. "Won't drinking coffee at this hour keep you awake?"

Tracy shook her head. "I'm completely immune. I drink so much coffee during the day to keep going that by the time night falls, its effects are completely neutralized." They were at his door. His arms were full of boy. She put out her hand. "Give me your key and I'll open the door."

He didn't have them handy. "They're in my pocket," he told her. She began to reach into his jacket pocket, but he shook his head. "No, my jeans pocket."

A sensual smile that made his gut tighten and then lurch lifted the corners of her mouth. "Maybe you'd better give me Jake. I don't think I know you well enough to frisk you yet."

He laughed quietly, relieved. Jake stirred as Adam handed him off to her.

Adam saw her eyes drift shut for a second as she drew the boy to her and held him against her. She looked as if she was savoring the moment. As if she was thinking of what might have been.

That was the way she was meant to be, he thought suddenly, holding a child in her arms. Empathy and sadness flooded him. He felt for her. Because of a cruel twist of fate, she would be denied a child of her own to hold the way she was holding Jake.

She could always adopt, he thought, taking out his key and unlocking the door.

Why hadn't she thought of that?

None of his business, he told himself sharply. He had to remember that there were lines to be adhered to, lines that shouldn't be crossed and he was not only thinking of crossing them, but of pole-vaulting right over them.

She was having a hell of an effect on him.

"I'll put him to bed," she volunteered, her voice just a little above a whisper as she entered the darkened apartment.

"Thanks."

Reaching into the room and feeling around on the wall, he flipped on a light. She went straight to the boy's room. He debated going with her, then decided to let her handle it on her own. He'd only get in her way and there was no doubt in his mind that she had it covered.

Right now, it seemed prudent to him to stay out of small, tight places if she was in them.

He looked around the kitchen, trying to remember where he kept his pots.

"Didn't open his eyes once," she announced several minutes later as she walked into the kitchen.

Adam was sitting at the small table. There were two cups of coffee out. Hers was light. He remembered that she took it with milk.

Impressed, Tracy raised her brows. "You made coffee."

"I made hot water," he corrected, nodding at the steaming pot standing on the stove. "Whatever's in that jar made coffee, such as it is."

She took a seat, noting by his tone that he preferred brewed to instant. Beggars couldn't exactly be choosers. "I'm not fussy. Besides, it's the thought that counts."

Lost in thoughts that he couldn't reveal, he didn't get the drift of her words. "The coffeemaker's?"

She smiled up into his eyes, amused. "If that's what you want to call yourself." She raised the cup to her lips, then set it back down again, afraid she was going to laugh into the liquid, spilling it. "I'm trying to thank you for being thoughtful."

"Not thoughtful," he denied. "You thought of it. You said you were inviting yourself over for coffee. I was just getting it ready while you put Jake to bed. Way I see it," he looked into her eyes, "you got the harder part of the deal."

The lengths he would go to in order to avoid accepting thanks truly astounded her. "Just let me say thank you, all right?"

He opened his mouth to negate the thanks, then shrugged. "All right." Never one to say more than he had to, he paused. Just this once, he decided to allow his dormant curiosity to take prisoners. Mainly him. "Why don't you adopt?"

Well, this certainly was out of the blue, she thought. "Adopt who? Jake?"

As usual, he wasn't making himself clear. If it didn't have to do with preventing fires or rescuing people, he found that he had a tendency to get tongue-tied. And she positively reduced his tongue to shreds.

"No, I mean in general." He wondered if she would tell him to mind his own business. She was within her rights to, but he felt he had to say this. Her expression before had been divided between beatific and ecstasy. "You really look as if being with kids is what matters most to you. If you can't have one of your own, why don't you adopt one?''

"I am with kids, all day long." No, that was being defensive, she upbraided herself. Adam didn't deserve that. He deserved an answer. "I'd like to get married first."

"Plenty of single women adopt these days." Although he doubted if she'd have much trouble finding a man willing to marry her.

"I know, but I feel that a child needs two parents whenever possible, not one." The smile on her face was rueful. "I wouldn't want to start out any child with a handicap."

"Seems to me that any kid who had you for a mother is as far from having a handicap as the earth is from the moon."

The look in her eyes thanked him far more eloquently than anything she could possibly say. The next moment, Adam saw tears shimmering in her eyes. It totally confused him.

Without even realizing he was doing it, Adam reached out and placed his hand over Tracy's in a gesture of comfort.

"Hey, I'm sorry. I didn't mean to make you cry."

Tracy wiped them away with the back of her hand, blinking to prevent any further onslaught from coming. "They're happy tears."

"That makes no sense at all." Tears were for sorrow, not joy.

She laughed, "Why should it? You're a man. Men don't understand tears unless they see a bullet wound.'' For the strong, silent type, he certainly had his moments. ''You really are very, very sweet.''

He could just hear the guys at the fire station hooting over that. ''You'd be the first to take up that point of view.''

Then everyone else was wrong, she thought. Because Adam Collins was very sweet. Irresistibly so. ''Well, you are.''

The need for her came slamming into him out of the shadows, like a punch that assailed him far too fast for him to duck out of the way.

So he took it on the chin. And tried not to lose his balance.

Adam rose from the table, his hand shifting so that his fingers now held hers. He drew Tracy up to her feet, drew her to him.

The next moment, his hands lightly cupping the back of her shoulders, he lowered his mouth to hers and kissed her.

The way he saw it, he had no choice.

Chapter 11

Her knees were the first to go.

Unsteady, Tracy grabbed onto his shoulders to anchor herself before she sank, ungracefully, to the ground. Her head began to spin, dangerously so, and she held onto him tightly, afraid to let go. Afraid that if she did, Adam would stop.

The kiss deepened. Layers, textures and all sorts of flavors, tantalizing and provocative, descended on her, overwhelming her. Making her forget time and space, making her forget everything but this wondrous moment in which the world held its breath as she had hers stolen from her.

A yearning came over her, a yearning with a grip so strong she didn't think she could pull free. She certainly couldn't walk away from it. Not without her knees. Or legs. Or any other part of her that might have been able to work at one time, but didn't at this precise moment. For right now, she was reduced to a state of liquid which was quickly reaching a dangerous boiling point.

She wanted him. Wanted Adam more than she wanted anything else at this moment.

Tracy didn't know what had come over her, why suddenly she had no willpower, no shame that it was gone. All she knew was that she wanted Adam to make love with her and if he didn't, she wasn't sure how she was going to survive until dawn.

He tasted her hunger. Or was that his own, echoing back to him?

Adam wasn't sure, didn't know how to find out. As the hunger grew, it ceased to matter whose it was, only that it was consuming him, body and soul.

Her breathing became audible to him, fanning the flames of his desire. Kissing her over and over again, he encircled his arms around her, drawing Tracy to him as if he meant to seal her against his body for all eternity.

Maybe he did. He wasn't sure now about any of his motives, except that they were dangerously out of control, threatening to take him hostage.

Her mouth tasted like wine, heady, intoxicating, creating a thirst within him rather than sating one. He went on kissing her as if he'd never get enough. Because it was true.

And then his lips left hers, devouring instead her cheeks, her chin, the tempting column of her throat, the sweet indentation just below her ear.

He felt as if he'd just been stumbling along in the dark these past two years and now he'd found his way. The idea was utterly absurd, but he couldn't shake free of it. Couldn't detach himself from the feeling that he had found home.

Adam knew he wouldn't be satisfied until Tracy was in his bed, twisting beneath him, twining her legs around his torso.

Maybe not even then.

The image jolted him, causing a temporary chasm. He struggled to regain at least a shred of control over himself. He succeeded. Marginally. It was enough for a valiant, gallant effort.

He pulled his head back from her. "Tracy?"

"Yes," she breathed, her voice echoing around his head, dancing along his skin.

It wasn't a question. It was an answer. Yes. From the bottom of her heart, yes.

To prove her intent and eliminate any doubt he might have, Tracy cupped his face between her hands and kissed him as if her entire soul was there, throbbing in her swollen lips.

He felt his pulse jump. Any defenses he might have had, any remaining thought at doing the honorable thing vanished.

He was hers.

Adam picked Tracy up in his arms and carried her into his bedroom. She wound her arms around his neck. He felt as if he could conquer the world right now. And yet, she had conquered him.

As quietly as he could, he pushed the door closed with his back.

"Lock it," she murmured against his ear, her breath sending long, hot shivers down his spine.

He knew she was right.

Setting her down, his body brushing against hers, Adam turned and carefully flipped the lock on his door. When he turned around again to say something to her, to perhaps give her one last chance to pull away, he never got the opportunity.

In that brief moment that he'd been otherwise occupied, Tracy had stripped off the sweater that had outlined her breasts so temptingly for him all day and evening and tossed it aside, along with her bra.

His mouth felt completely dry.

Adam could feel his lips curving in the first smile he'd felt from within in two years. Damn, but she was even more beautiful than in his fantasies. His hands slipped over her almost reverently.

"I guess you don't want me talking you out of this."

Heat was all but exploding in her veins. Tracy could feel his eyes touching her, caressing her. "No," she whispered, drawing closer to him, eliminating any space that existed between them.

He felt her breasts moving tantalizingly against his chest, creating a fierce hunger within him that gripped his belly. Quickly, he shed his shirt, throwing it to the floor.

The feel of her skin against his ignited a fire in his loins.

Combing his hands through her hair, cupping the back of her head, he kissed her mouth over and over again, unable to get enough. Afraid that this was just a dream and he would wake up. Or that the alarm would go off, calling him to a fire that was much too large for the station to handle.

But the only alarm that went off was within him, warning him that instead of fighting a fire, he was playing with one. He had no training for this, no experience to draw on. It was a fire so huge, it threatened to incinerate him without leaving a trace of his existence behind.

But that was all right with him. As long as it meant that he could have her, just once.

His hands felt large and clumsy as he undid the snap at her jeans. He saw excitement flicker in her eyes, could almost feel the tingle of excitement as she drew in her breath in anticipation.

The same anticipation that throbbed through him.

With his palms molded on either of her hips, Adam eased the denim from her body, working it down until the jeans were at her ankles. She stepped out of them and kicked them aside. He kneaded her bottom as he kissed her mouth, then his hands slipped beneath the silky material, a thrill weaving its way through him.

Over and over again, his mouth slanted across Tracy's, unable to get its fill, needing more and more of her with each passing second. He pushed her underwear down her body, pressing her warm, willing flesh to him.

He caught his breath as he felt her long, cool fingers work the zipper loose on his own jeans. Felt his loins humming with suppressed desire as she undid the snap.

Needs grew larger, assaulting him, threatening to

completely undo him. They slammed into him with blunt battering rams.

He wasn't sure how long he could hold himself back when all he could think about was taking her.

But he had to give her something, a part of himself. He couldn't just take her like some hormonal adolescent boy. As urgent as his needs were, he wanted her to remember this as something more than a random, heated coupling. He didn't do one-night stands and he didn't want her to think of this that way.

Shucking the jeans down and off his body, he began to remove his briefs. Her eyes on his, Tracy stayed his hands and slipped hers beneath them. Her fingers lightly passed over him through the cotton, possessing him.

His gut tightened like a quivering fist in one last scramble for control.

He shook his head in wonder.

"What?" she whispered, afraid that she had done something wrong.

Something deeper than desire stirred within him, but he ignored it, afraid to give it attention. Afraid to give it a name. He cupped his hand along her cheek.

"Woman, you know how to drive a man crazy in more ways than anyone can count."

"Who's counting?" she murmured, bringing her mouth up to his.

Entwined, their lips sealed against one another, they fell to the bed, seeking pleasure in a newly freed paradise they had both been afraid to enter.

Almost hesitant, Adam passed his hands over her nude, supple body. His desire was so urgent, he was afraid of hurting her. Afraid that if he touched her too hard, Tracy would melt away, like some dream he had that he wasn't meant to have.

She placed her hand over his as he caressed her breast, pressing his hand down. Holding it there.

"I won't break," she whispered against his mouth. "I promise."

The hoarsely whispered assurance seemed to be all he needed. The demands within him had reached almost a fever pitch. The kisses he rained upon her mouth and face, upon her throat and neck became more urgent until they could not be contained any longer.

Threading his fingers through hers, he rolled onto her. He poised himself over her and slowly, his mouth sealed to hers, Adam slid into her and sealed his body to her as well.

The rhythm overtook them both, drawing them seductively to that special place until they finally reached it.

Together.

His lungs bursting, his brain still encased in a haze, Adam felt himself drifting—not falling—to earth again. He heard the hammering of his heart as it lay against hers.

Or was that her heart hammering?

He didn't know. It didn't matter. For one brief second, they'd been one, shared one heart, one kiss, one moment of ecstasy. That was what counted.

He began to shift off her.

Her arms tightened around him in silent entreaty. "No," she murmured, "not yet."

The request, uttered so dreamily, made him smile again for the second time that evening. Part of him felt as if he'd drifted into some secret world of enchantment.

Gathering her against him, Adam moved so that he was pivoted up on his elbows and looking down into her face. He wasn't sure just what to say. What did you say to a woman who'd briefly opened up the door to a place you hadn't believed existed anymore?

"I'm hurting you," he said.

Not in a million years, she thought. "No, you're not. You're making me smile."

Guilt began to inch its way over him, cutting a path with a sharp, stiletto knife, cutting away his happiness. "I'm sorry."

She didn't understand. "For what?"

None of this should have happened. He'd just been unfaithful to the memory of a woman he thought he would always love. And he had no one to blame but himself. "I should have let you go home."

Let? It had been a long time since a man had "let" her do anything. The last man she'd allowed to have that kind of power over her was her father. She'd been underage at the time. Rebellion had kicked in soon afterward. As far back she could remember, she had always been her own person.

But she saw something in Adam's eyes she couldn't read, something that was blurred with sadness.

"I don't remember you locking the front door and me beating against it with my fists." He wasn't looking at her, his profile rigid. Tracy took his face in her hands and made him look at her. "This was mutual. Or, at least I think it was." She cocked her head. "Did I just have my way with you?"

Mischief entered her eyes a moment later.

Mischief that made her almost totally irresistible to him.

And made him want her all over again.

Adam didn't think that it was possible to want someone within three minutes of having them. What was it about this woman that reduced him to a mass of contradictions and question marks?

He hadn't a clue. All he knew were the demands his body was making on him, and right now that involved having her again.

"Maybe," he replied, then kissed her neck. He felt her move beneath him. Felt the urgency begin all over again, with even more intensity than the last time. "And maybe I'd like equal time."

"Equal time?" she breathed as tongues of fire began to lick at her again. "That sounds like it has possibilities. Just what did you have in mind?"

"This," he murmured, his breath warming her as he lowered his head and pressed his lips against the swell of her breast.

She made no attempt to restrain the moan that filled her, that escaped her lips as his tongue lightly passed over the hardened peak.

"And this," he told her, anointing the second breast as he had the first. "And maybe this."

His mouth trailed tantalizingly along her abdomen, making her belly quiver like a provocative harem dancer. She twisted and moved beneath him, taking his excitement and increasing it by twofold.

Eager, hungry all over again, Tracy arched against him as his lips branded her, making her his as surely as if she had been created that way. Cupping him, her fingers curving around his most sensitive region, Tracy rubbed her palm against him, enflaming him. Driving the game up to another level.

When he drove himself into her this time, she had to bite her lower lip to keep from crying out and possibly waking Jake up. Tracy entwined her legs around Adam's torso, cleaving to him tightly as they rode a second crest to the same sunrise they'd visited before.

He didn't remember falling asleep. Only vaguely remembered drawing Tracy to him to take comfort from her warmth.

There seemed to be something very right about holding this woman against him, about breathing in the light, heady fragrance of her hair and letting it lull him into a peacefulness that had escaped him the first time.

Maybe it wasn't peacefulness, maybe it was out and out exhaustion, he silently amended. He wasn't sure. But whatever it was, it kept the sadness that always haunted him at arm's length and for that he was eternally grateful.

But now daybreak was nudging its way into the room, making its presence known and the magic was even now ebbing away.

He really hadn't meant for it to go this far, he

thought, wondering how he could get out of this predicament.

His arm was trapped beneath her and he looked about for a way to ease it out without waking Tracy up. He really wasn't up to any kind of a conversation. He wasn't even sure how he felt about what had happened last night between them. Until he was, he didn't want to discuss it.

Ever so slowly, Adam began to work his arm out from beneath her.

"If you're trying to make a quiet getaway," her voice, husky and low, with sleep still framing each word, floated to him as it skimmed her pillow, "I think I should point out that you're the one who lives here."

She turned around, pulling the sheet to her breasts. Reminding him of the warm, supple body that was just beneath. Her eyes were flirting with him.

"'Morning."

So much for a smooth exit. He passed his tongue over his lips. "'Morning," he muttered.

Tracy sat up, freeing his trapped arm. He pulled it away as if he thought she was going to pin him down again. She cocked her head, trying to read him. "*Were* you trying to make a getaway?"

"I was trying not to wake you." Which was the truth, as far as it went.

"Considerate and a fantastic lover. What a combination." Her eyes washed over him. There was mischief in them, just as there had been last night.

If anyone deserved a compliment, it was her. "You were pretty fantastic yourself."

She laughed softly to herself, her eyes never leaving his. "I guess we both rose to the occasion."

A corner of the sheet drooped, allowing him just the barest hint of a view of her breast. Enough to whet his appetite. And then some.

If he didn't get moving now, he was going to slip back into bed with her and make love again, a little voice warned.

Tracy glanced at her watch, the only thing she hadn't taken off last night. It was six o'clock in the morning. A sense of responsibility reared its head somewhat belatedly.

"Oh God, Petunia's probably eating the rug." On her feet, completely unselfconscious in her nudity, Tracy began to gather up her clothes. "I've got to get home and feed her."

He couldn't help himself.

The sight of her body, seductively shadowed in the dusky early morning, was too much for him. He couldn't even try to resist.

Coming up behind her as she started to get dressed, Adam turned her around to face him. And then he kissed her again.

Tracy's good intentions melted with her resolve.

"Well, maybe a few more minutes won't hurt," she murmured. After all, it wasn't as if she'd left the animal to starve. She'd made sure Petunia had a heaping dish of pet food in her dish before she'd left yesterday morning. "I'll give her an extra portion when I get home. Roasted ears of corn with truffles. Her favorite."

It was all she could say. Her mouth was suddenly too busy to form words.

Chapter 12

Adam had no idea how it evolved, but thoughts of Tracy were filling his days and his nights.

He'd actually made himself believe, after that first night they'd spent together, that it was just a one-time thing, that it was better for both of them that way. That if he didn't say anything to her and steered clear of the subject, the night of passionate lovemaking would be forgotten.

Instead, though he had valiantly kept up his side of the silent bargain he'd made with himself, that night was always there, in the back of his mind, whispering seductively to him. Making him ache to recapture the moments. To duplicate them. The memory of that night dictated his movements, dominated his mind, gave him no peace.

After more than a week, he stopped waiting for it to fade and stopped secretly hoping that fate would arrange things so that the decision to be with her would be somehow taken out of his hands and forced upon him by one event or another. After nine days of trying to remain civil but distant, Adam became a mover again, rather than a bystander in his own life.

As they went through their own changing of the guard ever since he had gone back to duty and she to her position in the hospital, Adam took matters into his own hands. About to leave for work, he stopped Tracy before she could go to check in on Jake. The boy was in his bedroom, playing with a video game set she had recently bought for him. After some coaxing, Jake started to play. Now it seemed to be the only thing that grounded him.

Surprised that Adam stopped her, she raised her brow in a silent query. Silence, it seemed, was not a mode restricted to Jake alone. Adam apparently preferred it himself.

"I need to talk to you."

Tracy could feel her heart pick up its tempo. They'd hardly spoken more than nine sentences in as many days. She was beginning to think that anything she'd felt that single night they'd shared had been one-sided. The following day, he'd acted as if it had never happened and she would be damned if she was going to be the one to bring it up. Up to that point, she had to admit she'd done almost everything except trip him and stand on his chest to bring him around. But some things a woman had to let a man do or it just didn't count.

Tracy wasn't altogether certain she liked the tone of his voice. Was he going to tell her he wanted to erase her from his life? Or maybe he wanted her to know he was going to give Jake back to the foster system that was still attempting, along with his lawyer, to untangle the matter of his guardianship? His expression gave nothing away. The man was just as much of a trial to her as the boy. More so.

Second-guessing was giving her a headache. "Yes?" she prodded.

Adam felt as if his tongue had turned into a giant, hot omelet that was almost impossible to handle. Words weren't coming. Frustrated, he said the obvious. "I have to go on duty tonight."

"I know that." Tracy waited for him to tell her something she didn't know.

Damn, but she was making this hard, looking at him with those soft hazel eyes of hers. "But I don't have to tomorrow."

This was beginning to sound odd. "I know that, too." He'd given her his schedule last week. He knew that. What was this about?

Pressing her lips together to keep her questions back, she waited for Adam to continue. After all, he'd started this conversation, such as it was.

But when no more words followed, she leaped to the only conclusion she could. "If you're trying to tell me not to come over, you don't have to. I know the arrangement."

He blew out an exasperated breath. For once he wished that he had the glib ways of his brothers. Especially Dennis. Dennis always knew what to say no matter what the situation.

"No," he finally said, "I'm trying to tell you *to* come over."

She decided he couldn't mean what she'd like him to mean. This was Adam and Adam wanted no involvement. He'd made that perfectly clear. "Because you're going out?" she guessed.

He didn't know how much plainer he could make this without tripping on his tongue again. "No, because I'm staying in."

She'd had shoes that were more communicative than this man was. "I bet they called you 'Gabby' when you were a kid."

Adam cleared his throat and made another attempt. "I'm trying to ask you to come over because I'm staying in." His eyes held hers for the briefest of seconds. "Come for dinner. I'll cook this time. Grilled steaks," he elaborated. The impact of what he'd just said hit him. Maybe she'd misunderstood his motives. He dragged a hand through his hair. "Look Tracy, I can't promise you anything—"

One step at a time, she cautioned herself. *Like with Jake, take this one step at a time.* "I never asked you to," she told him quietly.

He went on as if she hadn't interjected anything. Now that he'd started this, she deserved to know the rest of it. "—But I can't seem to get you out of my head."

Was that fear she saw in his eyes, or wariness? "And that's a bad thing?"

"I don't know," he told her honestly.

She smiled, her heart warming. This had taken a

lot on his part, she knew that. "Maybe you should try to find out."

He squared his shoulders, feeling not unlike someone sharing military plans with the enemy. Maybe he was crazy. All he knew was that trying to avoid her wasn't working.

"That's what I'm going to be doing. Tomorrow night." He shrugged, afraid that she might make more of this than it was—even though he wasn't sure himself just *what* it was. "Besides, you're so much better talking to Jake than I am." He looked at her. "I need input," he confessed.

Tracy couldn't help laughing. "You need a ventriloquist," she corrected. "Maybe you haven't noticed but most conversations I have with you are eighty percent monologues. You have a tendency to act as if you came from the Gary Cooper School of Communication. All you need to do is kick the ground a few times and mumble, 'Shucks, ma'am,' and you'd be a shoo-in."

He tried to find his way in this maze he found himself in. "So is that a no, you won't come?"

Her mouth curved in a fond smile as she shook her head. The man couldn't read her at all, could he?

"No, that's a yes." Unable to stop herself, she touched his cheek. In his own strange way, the man was a dear. "Haven't you heard? I'm a sucker for Gary Cooper. Saw all his movies as a kid."

He looked at Tracy uncertainly. "Hasn't he been dead for a long time?"

"Cable has an awful lot of old movie channels," she reminded him. The man probably never even turned on his set when he was alone, she guessed. Which made him very different than her. After greeting Petunia, she always turned on her set just for the comforting sound of voices talking in the background. ''You'd be surprised what's on late at night for a lonely kid to watch.''

He had to get going, even though the fire station was only a few blocks from his apartment. Yet he wanted to linger, to hear her speak. Having abandoned his futile attempt to root her out of his mind, both subconscious and otherwise, he now wanted to remain and talk with her.

Hell, he upbraided himself, call a spade a spade. He didn't want to talk with her, he wanted to make love with her. Wildly. All night.

And feeling this way scared the hell out of him.

With effort, he shook himself free of the thought. This wasn't the time or the place. He had work to get to and Jake was awake.

Adam began to edge out of the room and toward the door. But his eyes remained on her. What she'd said had caught his attention.

''Were you? A lonely kid I mean?'' he asked when she didn't respond immediately.

She nodded. ''Pretty much. My parents didn't approve of too many people.'' Well-to-do with superior intellects, her parents were utter snobs and completely unapproachable. ''That limited my access to anyone. They thought I would do better to read and improve my mind instead of wasting my time playing with other kids.''

He would have thought that someone who was

raised like that wouldn't be able to relate to children, would be more of a loner, like him. Yet he was the one with a basketful of siblings and a large extended family and he liked keeping to himself for the most part. Especially after fate had twisted a knife in his gut.

Funny how things turned out.

He realized that if he remained here one more second, looking into her eyes, he was going to sweep her into his arms and kiss her. And more than likely set fire to all his good intentions.

In self-defense, he glanced at his watch. "I'd better go. I don't want to be late."

"Can't tarnish a perfect record," she couldn't help teasing.

"Right."

Adam was halfway out the door before he stopped and doubled back. Good intentions or not, he knew he couldn't just walk out like this. Not when there was this need building up within him like some kind of coal-fed railroad engine. Catching hold of her waist with one hand, he pulled Tracy to him and kissed her hard before finally releasing her.

Without a word, he turned on his heel and left, knowing that he was precariously close to throwing all caution to the wind.

Tracy ran the tip of her tongue lightly along her lips. Tasting him. She stared after Adam, more than a little mystified and dazed. And more than a little happy.

"You are a puzzlement, Adam Collins, that you

are,'' she murmured. But it was a puzzle she meant to find the solution to.

With that, she went to look in on Jake.

He wasn't altogether sure that he was doing the right thing. A dozen trite sayings ran through his head, from ''Let sleeping dogs lie'' to the equally spectacular ''If it ain't broke, don't fix it.'' All of them undermined his decision to have Tracy over for dinner.

If he continued to sail along, he argued silently as he threw cherry tomatoes onto some fresh lettuce, avoiding all but the most cursory encounters with Tracy, perhaps eventually he would get back to the place he'd been before he met her.

Dumping a glob of Caesar dressing on the combination, he began mixing everything together.

Yeah, right, and maybe the sun would start orbiting around the earth.

It wasn't going to happen. He wasn't going to find his way, blindly or otherwise, to square one and he might as well make his peace with that.

Setting the salad bowl aside on the counter, Adam opened the oven door and pulled the pan halfway out. Gingerly, he turned the three steaks he was broiling over with his large fork.

As he closed the door again, he saw the boy looking at him curiously. Jake had been hanging around the perimeter of the kitchen for the past ten minutes, watching him.

''Yes, she's coming.''

He was getting pretty good at reading Jake, at anticipating the questions that were not going to be verbalized.

Adam knew he'd guessed correctly when the boy smiled. It was a Tracy smile, Adam thought. The smile that Jake wore whenever the woman did something to please him. It wasn't difficult. The boy was coming along, eating better, playing games. Listening when she read to him. Even watching that silly little pig of hers when she brought it over to do tricks. Adam could have sworn he almost laughed out loud when she showed the boy the way her pet could find her when she hid in closets or behind doors.

Maybe soon, he thought. Maybe soon Jake would talk again.

He wondered what Jake's laugh *was* like. Was it like hers? Light and airy, or did it sound like a high-pitched belly laugh, the way his nephew's did?

Examining and discarding several, Adam finally dug out three paper napkins that didn't look as if someone had sat on them. He placed them on the table.

"Wish I knew what you were thinking, Jake. Wish I knew how to unlock whatever lock snapped shut for you."

Frustrated, he pushed the thought out of his head. Nothing was going to change tonight so there was no use in belaboring things he had no control over.

Like the way he was beginning to feel about Tracy.
Beginning.

The word mocked him, as if he knew that he was lying to himself.

Well, hadn't he been lying to himself all along,

thinking that he couldn't feel anything for anyone again? That everything he was or would ever be had died along with Gloria? He hadn't died and maybe that was what he regretted the most. He was alive and well and every passing day made him that much more acutely aware of that fact.

That he felt.

But he couldn't dwell on it.

"Get me the milk out of the refrigerator, will you Jake?" he asked as he put the appropriate flatware on the table.

Glancing over his shoulder, he saw the boy making his way to the refrigerator.

To look at Jake, you would never have thought anything was wrong. He looked like an average, healthy five-year-old. Except that he still didn't speak.

But there was life to him now and color to his cheeks, unlike when he'd gone to see Jake in the hospital or when he'd first brought him home. That was entirely Tracy's doing, Adam thought.

He smiled to himself. Tracy had a way of breathing life into the lifeless.

He was living proof.

The doorbell rang as he put down the last fork on the small kitchen table. It barely accommodated the three of them, but luckily, Jake was small and didn't require much room.

He saw Jake looking at him expectantly.

"That's her," Adam told the boy even as he crossed to the door. The boy took a step back, waiting. His eyes intent on the door.

Adam pulled it open.

She looked different, he thought. And then it hit him. She was wearing a dress. She looked the way she might if she were going out on a date.

Is that what this was? A date? He couldn't wrap his mind around that.

And he couldn't take his eyes off her. The electric blue sheath slid along her curves the way his hands itched to do.

He needed a cold shower. But it was too late for that.

"Can I take that from you?" he asked, nodding at the grocery bag she was holding.

"My arms haven't gone numb, Collins," she informed him cheerfully, breezing past him and walking in. "Mrs. Wells looked as if she approved."

"You talked to her?" he asked, shutting the door.

"No, but she smiled when I waved to her." Tracy saw Jake standing next to the counter. "There's the light of my life. How are you doing, Jake?" The smile on his face, albeit tiny, caused triumph to course through her veins. *Baby steps.* She set the bag down on the counter, then bent over to kiss the top of the boy's head. "He been treating you okay?" For the boy's benefit, she nodded toward Adam. "Can't complain, huh? Well, you can if you want to," she advised, slipping off her coat and tossing it onto a recliner in the living room, beside Adam's and Jake's. For some reason neither one of them understood, Jake wanted to keep his jacket there, close to the door. So that was where they left it, along with theirs, to give the boy a feeling of unity.

"Just tug on my sleeve anytime you're ready and

we'll have a heart-to-heart about this big, strapping fireguy.'' She stopped to sniff the air. ''Is that dinner?''

Adam tore his eyes away from the back of her dress, which dipped down halfway to her waist and made him realize that she couldn't be wearing a bra. It took a second before he could reply.

''Yes, and it's not burning if that's what you're going to say. It's grilling.''

Her grin was broad, humoring. ''Of course it is. I never doubted it for a moment.'' she stepped over to the stove. ''Mind if I take a look?''

Before he could say anything about the sacred firefighter tradition of meat grilling, Tracy was opening the oven door.

He shook his head. The woman did have a way of taking over. ''Would it stop you if I said yes?''

Bending over to examine the steaks, Tracy smiled at him over her shoulder. She gave dinner the once-over. ''It might give me pause.''

''But then you'd just sail on.''

She closed the oven door and straightened up. ''Me? Wouldn't dream of it.''

Tracy moved over to the counter and took out the two bottles she had brought with her. There was one bottle of red wine to go with the grilled steaks Adam told her he was making, and one bottle of sparkling grape juice for Jake.

''Brought you your own bottle,'' she told the boy. ''That way you can join us.'' She winked at Jake. Then, turning to Adam, who made no secret that he was watching her every move, she asked, "Anything you want me to do?"

The answers that came to him couldn't be voiced in front of Jake. As a matter of fact, for his own sake, they were better left unsaid. He'd already sunk himself in deeper than he'd intended by inviting her over for dinner.

He glanced toward the kitchen table he'd covered with a red tablecloth not fifteen minutes ago. There was a large stain just beneath his own plate. "You can finish setting the table."

"Sounds good to me. Want to help, Jake?" She took out three glasses from the cupboard—the only three Adam had, she noted—and handed them to the boy one at a time. "You know, Jake, back in the very old days, before they had fire trucks, whenever they had a fire, the people of the town would form a fire line from a horse trough to wherever the fire was. The person at the back of the line would fill a bucket with water and pass it on to the next person and so on until the bucket reached the first person in line who was standing by the burning building. He got to be the one to throw the bucket of water at the fire. They just kept on passing buckets of water until the fire was out."

Or the building was gone, Adam thought.

"This is kind of like a fire line, except that it's just you and me." She saw Jake glance toward Adam. "Well, I guess he's our very own fireguy, yours and mine. Isn't that neat?"

The boy said nothing, but the man looked at her in

a way that made her feel as if her kneecaps were going to be in danger of melting again. And soon.

She could hardly wait.

Nerves drummed urgently through him, as did a sense of uneasiness. Knowing there was no way to avoid it, Bancroft peered into Stone's office. He'd hoped to leave for the night without any incident, but Hernandez had told him that Stone was looking for him.

That couldn't be good.

But if he avoided him, it would become even worse. He licked his thin lips and tried to sound as if he wasn't a man walking a tightrope.

"You wanted to see me, Chief?"

Throwing down the latest report on the possible suspects behind the bombing at the country club, Stone glared at the man in his doorway. Rumors were still flying right and left, rumors that put the blame on the Mexican Mafia, disgruntled members and random terrorists. He could live with that if those were the only suspects. But they weren't. He'd heard whispers that there might be dirty cops behind the bombing.

He couldn't afford to let that rumor spread. He needed to wipe it out at its source. Trouble was, he didn't know where the source was. But he had his suspicions.

"I am tired of feeling as if I'm sitting on some kind of a powder keg, Bancroft, dangling my feet over the side while I'm waiting for it to go off." He rose, pushing away from his desk. "That kid's been out of the hospital for almost two weeks. That's over four weeks since the accident happened. He's gotta be talking by now. I want you to go back to him tomorrow and see what he knows. He's staying with that firefighter who rescued him. Adam Collins.'' He saw the uneasy look in the other man's eyes. ''Get a backbone, Goddamn it. You're a cop. This is an ongoing investigation, isn't it? You're part of the task force, aren't you? You want that hotshot female Molly French to get a bee in her bonnet and try to coax a few words out of the kid? I can't control her. If she finds out anything or puts things together, it might mean the end of everything.''

''But what if Collins is there? He didn't let us near the kid in the hospital.''

''He's a firefighter. He's gone two days in a row. Hell, don't you know anything?'' he demanded in disgust. ''Get to the kid then.''

''What if he still can't talk?''

Stone didn't believe in this mute act, but he wouldn't rest until it became a reality. ''I like my witnesses silent,'' the chief told him, his meaning clear. ''Permanently.''

A wave of nausea came over Bancroft and his skin turned clammy. His stomach tightening into a knot, he felt like throwing up. He said nothing.

Chapter 13

"Leave them."

Jake had fallen asleep to the misadventures of one of Dr. Seuss's characters, the way Bobby always did when he'd read the stories to his son at bedtime. Adam had emerged from Jake's room to find that not only had Tracy straightened up the living room and, with the exception of the jackets on the armchair next to the door, put everything away, but that she was now in the kitchen, wrestling with the pan that had contained the grilled streaks.

After seeing the condition of the pan, Adam had decided it would be easier just to throw it away and buy a new one than waste energy cleaning it. He'd told her as much.

Spoken like a true man, she thought fondly. As if dishes, like cats, washed themselves. She continued battling the burned-on grease in the pan. "I hate dirty dishes piling up in the sink. They tend to multiply."

Standing behind her, Adam breathed in her scent. And felt anticipation begin to hum through his veins. It was all he could do not to encircle her waist and draw her against him. But if he did that, this time he might not make it to the bedroom with her. And there was Jake to think about.

"They're not rabbits, and I don't have any more dishes so they can't multiply." Taking her hand, he drew her away from the sink and turned her around. No matter how he struggled, how much he tried to hang on to common sense and tell himself that there was no future here, there wasn't a single inch of him that didn't want her. "You know, I'm trying not to have any feelings for you."

Now there was a line destined not to make the dating circuit, Tracy thought. She raised her eyes to his. "How are you doing?"

He sighed, touching just her hair. "Failing miserably."

The smile in her eyes reached out to him. "Is that why you asked me over to dinner?"

He couldn't tell her anything but the truth. "I asked you over because I missed you. Because all I can think about is making love with you."

At least they were on the same page, she thought, relieved. "A nice, honest approach." The smile turned into a grin. "A little threadbare on the sweet talk, but honest."

That was just the point. She deserved someone who could give her things he couldn't, tell her things that didn't even occur to him to say. "I can't sweet-talk you, Tracy. I can't be anything but what I am."

She shook her head. He still didn't understand, did he? "No one is asking you to be anything else."

But for her, he should be. Still, there was a world of difference between what was and what should be. The least he could do is let her know something about the man who was becoming involved with her. Let her know the heartache that would always be his. "I never told you I had a son—"

There was that word again. Had. "You didn't have to. I sort of put the pieces together."

"Did you also put together the pieces that he and his mother died because I couldn't save them?"

There was such anguish in his eyes when he looked at her, it wrenched her heart. She wanted to reach out to him, to hold him and somehow make it dissipate, even a little. But something told her he had to get this out before it ate him alive.

"Go on."

"It happened while I was on duty at the fire station. I had already pulled on my gear before I heard the address. My address. I got there too late." He looked up at the ceiling, wishing for the countless time that things had been different.

"You weren't the only one," she pointed out. "There were other firefighters."

"There was faulty wiring in the master closet. I should have checked that."

"You couldn't have known."

"It was my *job* to know." It hurt to breathe as he spoke. "I couldn't reach either one of them."

This time, she did put her arms around him. "I'm so sorry, Adam."

He nodded. He knew she was. He took stock of himself. He hadn't asked her here to unload on her. He'd asked her here because she was warm and he needed her warmth. Adam looked into her eyes. "I don't know if I can give you what you want."

The man overthought the situation too much. She was a firm believer that what would be, would be. "Let's just enjoy the moment and not talk about the future."

It was a nice, safe plan and though he felt it was cowardly, he took refuge in it.

In her.

Taking her hand again, he led Tracy into his bedroom and closed the door, flipping the lock. The "click" resounded in the room, framed by the sound of their breathing.

The echo of their desire.

She stood beside his bed, watching him. Waiting for him to make the first move. He crossed to her, almost afraid to touch her. Afraid that he was dreaming, the way he had been all the other nights.

"You look nice in a dress," he murmured, his breath touching her face, caressing her even before his hands did. "You'd look nicer out of it."

To prove it, Adam brushed his lips against hers as he reached behind her back. Very slowly, he pulled the zipper down to its source. A thrill skated down his spine. He kissed her again, more deeply than before, as he drew the material away from her shoulders, letting it fall to the floor.

She wasn't wearing a bra. Just as he'd surmised. All she had on, besides her high heels, was the barest lacy white thong.

His heart went into overdrive the instant he drew back and saw it.

He'd never seen anyone more seductive. ''Did you wear that for me?''

''I don't wear anything for you,'' she whispered softly against his mouth as she kissed him.

Already hazing over with intoxication that had nothing to do with the glass of wine he'd had at dinner, it took a second for Adam's brain to grasp what Tracy was actually saying to him. That she wore nothing for him.

And nothing never looked better.

He couldn't go slowly, though he wanted to. He wanted to anoint every part of her, to touch, fondle, explore every inch of Tracy's body again with the worshipful reverence of an archeologist with a precious new find, but his body was pleading with him to take her. To make wild, passionate love with her before the moment, and his courage, deserted him.

Adam pulled off his shirt, throwing it aside, then unbuckled his belt and undid the snap at his jeans, his lips barely breaking contact with hers. He'd never felt this eager before, not even the first night they'd spent together. It was because he knew what was coming.

Still wearing the thong and her heels, Tracy laughed softly against his mouth. ''In a hurry, are we?''

He didn't answer.

Instead, naked, he wrapped his arms around her and kissed her hard.

Tracy felt as if the top of her head was about to come off. It certainly felt as if she was spinning out of control.

She didn't remember falling onto the bed, didn't take note of anything except the deep, consuming hunger that began deep in the pit of her belly and fanned outward to all her extremities. Her desperation, she discovered in surprise, matched his.

Her hands swept over his hard body, exploring him as he explored her. Possessing him as he possessed her. Their bodies twisted together as the heat that emerged all but fused them to one another.

And then, dragging what was left of her wits together, Tracy surprised him. Moving so that she had Adam flat on his back, she straddled him, her thighs forming a sensual parenthesis around his hips.

Adam found himself breathing harder as desire grew to tremendous proportions. His eyes caressed her face. "I can count the seconds since I had you."

"Wrong," she whispered as she began to move seductively over him. "We had each other."

Her eyes never leaving his, Tracy coaxed him into her. Then, as he gripped her hips, she began to move. Faster and faster as they climbed up to the summit.

Adam grasped her arms, pulling her down to him, covering her mouth urgently with his half a heartbeat before he crested. The gasp he heard against his lips told him he hadn't reached journey's end alone.

And then she was pouring her body over his like warm, soothing liquid, laying against him utterly boneless. He held her to him, gently stroking her hair. "You are a constant source of surprise to me."

Exhausted, she turned her head so that she could nip at his lower lip. He felt her smile curving against his chest and then she was running the tip of her tongue over his lower lip.

She could feel him reacting. A confident, glowing smile slipped over her lips as she raised her head, pushing back her hair from her face. "Do you want to surprise me?"

He knew what she was saying. She wanted to make love again. Exhaling a mighty breath, he laughed. "Why don't you give me a minute?"

She was moving against him again, her hips brushing along his as she pressed a kiss to his Adam's apple.

He felt his eyes fluttering shut. "Maybe half a minute," he amended. Adam felt her mouth making its way up to his chin. Shock waves vibrated through him. His loins pulsed with renewed desire. "Oh, the hell with it. Time's up."

His arms around her, he turned Tracy so that they reversed their positions. It was his turn to drive her crazy.

He did it with aplomb.

Adam hung up the phone, fighting the kind of disappointment that went with the career he had chosen. Captain MacIntire had called to inform him that a particularly nasty strain of flu was going around. Five firefighters had called in sick this morning. He was needed at the station to make up the complement.

Knowing the situation with Jake, the captain had promised that it was only for half a day, that the call was in to others to pick up some of the slack. There was no way he could refuse to do his part. At least MacIntire had the good grace to apologize for ruining his plans.

Adam heard the key in the lock. He'd given his spare to Tracy. She'd left to make a quick trip to her apartment to get a change of clothes and bring Petunia over for Jake to play with. She was hoping that the friendly pet would succeed in drawing him all the way out.

"We're here," she announced, bending over to deposit the potbellied pig on the floor. Rising, she took one look at Adam's face and knew something had happened. "What's wrong?"

The woman completely astounded him. He shook his head. "You're good."

She gave a careless half shrug. "I'm in tune with people." She stepped around Petunia, crossing to him. "Don't change the subject, what's wrong?" Since he wasn't around, she looked toward the boy's bedroom. "Is it Jake?"

But Adam shook his head. "Captain MacIntire just called."

She knew what that meant. "You have to go in."

She didn't sound upset, he thought. That was odd. Gloria had always gotten so upset every time his job got in the way of any of their plans. "Just for the morning."

Tracy nodded. "Go. Jake and I will entertain each

other. I'll show him some more of my sleight-of-hand tricks. He seems to like that.''

It was something she'd perfected when she was younger. Specifically, she'd shoplifted in a vain attempt to get her parents' attention. What it had gotten her was a severe reprimand from a kindly store manager and an even more severe case of guilt and shame. Her parents never even acknowledged the incident.

He studied her face, looking for any visible signs of annoyance. There weren't any. ''You're not angry?''

''Disappointed, maybe,'' she allowed. She dug into her pocket and tossed a truffle toward Petunia, who devoured it before it could hit the ground. She grinned at the pet. ''But I've had enough emergencies of my own. The next beeper that goes off could be mine,'' she reminded him.

And then Tracy raised herself up on her toes and kissed him quickly on the lips, drawing back before the kiss could flower into something more tempting. She was having trouble letting him go as it was.

''Go,'' she told him pushing him toward the door. She picked up his jacket from where it lay next to Jake's. She tossed her purse over beside it. It listed to one side, emptying out. ''Be brave. Save someone.''

He pulled his jacket on, then caught her hand. There was a warmth budding within him, a warmth that had nothing to do with temperature, or even the promise of another torrid night of lovemaking ahead. It exclusively had to do with the woman standing before him. He never thought he would feel this way again.

"It's you who's saved me," he told her. And then, brushing his lips against hers quickly, he hurried out the door.

Tracy sighed, staring at the closed door. "That man has some exit lines." She turned around to see that the pig had made a beeline for Jake, who'd come out of his room, drawn by the sound of her voice. "She is really getting very, very fond of you."

Crossing to the sofa, Tracy sat down and patted the space beside her, waiting for Jake to join her. He wiggled onto the sofa, his small feet sticking out before him like two unsynchronized windshield wipers, moving madly back and forth.

"I can see the feeling is mutual." She grinned, a faraway memory teasing her mind. She struggled to capture it, but only fragments returned. "You know, when I was a very little girl, I can remember someone playing a silly game with me. Did your mom ever do this?" Moving one of his feet closer to her, she lightly tweaked his big toe, then systematically moved on to the rest. "This little piggy went to market, this little piggy stayed home. This little piggy had roast beef and this little piggy had none—poor piggy,' she commented with a wink. "And this little piggy cried wee-wee-wee—"

"All the way home."

Tracy's mouth fell open. She stared at Jake, her heart beginning to pound. After more than a month of silence, he'd uttered his first word, his first phrase.

"You talked. Jake, you talked." She threw her

arms around him and hugged hard, tears welling up in her eyes. She kissed the top of his head as she rocked with him. "Oh baby, you talked."

"My mom used to do that," he told her, his voice muffled with emotion and hoarse from disuse. When he raised his head, his eyes were brimming with tears. They spilled out onto his small cheeks. "She's never going to do that again, is she?"

"No, baby, she's not. But she's watching over you right now. And so is your dad. They'll always be with you in your heart."

Gathering him to her, Tracy held him for a long time as he cried out all the pain he had been holding back for all these weeks. Rocking, she murmured over and over again, "Cry it out, honey, its going to be okay," while Petunia milled about close to him, as if sensing that something was amiss.

Finally, she heard Jake say, "I saw them."

Still holding her to him, her heart quickened. "Your parents?" That would be terrible, if he had seen their charred bodies lying there.

"No, men. I thought they were Santa's helpers, but they were bad men."

Not knowing if he was mixing reality with nightmares, Tracy drew him back from her breast in order to hear him more clearly.

"They were dragging big bags outside from the room. They were throwing the bags into a truck and they got mad when they saw me," he remembered. His mouth turned down. "I was just looking."

None of this was making any sense to her. It had to be a nightmare. But he looked so adamant, she pretended that it had really happened. "Jake, honey, what men? Where were you?"

"I was trying to find the bathroom. Mommy didn't want me to go by myself, but Daddy said I was a big boy. I was trying not to get lost," he insisted, his eyes searching her face to see if she believed him. "There was a door opened to this big room—"

He was saying the words all in a rush, as if they'd been trying to escape all this time. She had to slow him down. "What room, honey? The bathroom?"

He shook his head so hard, his blond hair bounced about his face. "No, it was a room with lots and lots of TVs. But there were no cartoons on. Just empty rooms. The man yelled at me when he saw me."

The security room, she realized suddenly. He was talking about the Lone Star Country Club. Adam had told her that he'd found the boy some distance from the Grill. Had he passed the security room on his way to the bathroom? She wasn't familiar with the club's layout.

What was it that he'd seen that had him so agitated? And why had the door been slammed in the boy's face? Was it just a precautionary measure, or was there something that someone hadn't wanted him to see?

"What kind of bags, honey?" she prodded, trying to get to the bottom of this. It was probably nothing, but the task force had sent two policemen to question him in the hospital. Maybe all this tied together somehow.

"Big ones. There was something green..." He tried hard to remember, but he couldn't. Jake shook his head in defeat and put his hand to his throat. "It feels all rough and scratchy."

The doctor in her superseded the curious woman. He could tell her about this all later.

"That's because you haven't used it in so long. Some nice warm chocolate milk'll make it feel a whole lot better," she promised.

Getting up, she crossed to the kitchen and conducted a swift search of Adam's cupboards. Nothing. She might have known.

She let the last cupboard door drop into place. "Except that Mr. Fireguy doesn't have any. Tell you what, why don't we go out and I'll treat you to some?" She could use a large cup of hot coffee that didn't come out of a glass jar herself, she thought. "Put your shoes on, Jake. We're going out."

He didn't have to be told twice. Plopping down on the floor, he began to put on his electric blue tennis shoes. Petunia came close to offer her assistance.

"Now where did I put my purse?" she muttered under her breath. Spying it on the chair tucked against Jake's jacket, she went over to pick it up. The shoulder bag had fallen on its side, the contents closest to the top spilling out haphazardly. It was always doing that, she thought in disgust. She needed a smaller purse.

As she started to shove things back into it, the doorbell rang. She put her purse down on the floor, leaning it against the side of the armchair and looked at Jake.

"You expecting company?" When he shook his head, she looked at Petunia. "How about you? Any-

one coming by to see you?'' Jake giggled. The sound
warmed her heart even as the doorbell pealed again.
''So that's what your laugh sounds like. Nice,'' she
told him.

''Thanks.'' He beamed at her. ''I like the way you
laugh, too.''

Her hand on the doorknob, Tracy inclined her head
by way of a silent thanks. Then, opening the door,
she completely froze.

It was one of the two officers who had come to the
hospital to question Jake. Something deep down
within her felt uneasy.

She made no attempt to open the door any wider.
''Hello Officer—'' she paused, reading his badge,
''Bancroft.'' Tracy raised her eyes back to his face.
''What brings you by here?''

Bancroft peered into the apartment, trying to see.
''I've come by to see how the boy's doing and if he's
up to answering questions yet. Mind if I come in?''
He didn't wait for her permission but shouldered his
way into the kitchen. ''Thanks,'' he mumbled at her,
continuing to scan the area. He saw Jake. Petunia had
shuffled off, out of view. ''Hi, kid, how're you doing?''

Instead of answering, Jake instantly became shy
and drew closer to Tracy.

There was a flicker of recognition in Jake's eyes,
coupled with apprehension that was not lost on Tracy.
But whether it was because he recognized the policeman from the time in the hospital when he'd first
come to question him or for some other reason, she
didn't know.

And then she remembered. Some of the policemen on the force moonlighted for extra money as security guards at the country club. Could Bancroft be one of the "bad men" Jake had seen transferring the bags from the security room to the truck? There was no way to tell at the moment.

All she knew was that she didn't want the policeman in the apartment.

She took Jake's hand and gave it a reassuring squeeze. "I'm afraid he's still not talking."

Bancroft looked at the boy suspiciously. "I heard voices when I came up to the door."

"That was the television set," Tracy told him innocently.

He looked in the direction of the television. "It's not on."

Tracy never lost a beat. "I just turned it off when I came to answer the door. And I was also talking to Jake." She pretended to think for a second. "That might have been what you heard."

His eyes darted to the boy and then back at her. "I thought you said he couldn't talk."

She looked at him as if he were being humorously naive. "Just because a woman doesn't get an answer doesn't mean she stops talking."

Frustration and aggravation got the better of Bancroft. There was a great deal at stake here. If the boy knew anything, anything at all, if there was a way he could communicate what he knew, then he could point fingers. Investigations could start in earnest. With people other than the members of Stone's Lion's Den handling the questioning.

Any way you looked at it, things could get ugly and quickly get out of hand. Stone's neck could be on the line and if Stone's head was in jeopardy of being lopped off, then so was his. And he was more afraid of Stone than he was of the authorities. The authorities would only send him to prison. Stone would do worse than that.

The boy had seen something, whether he knew what he saw or not didn't matter. He was a threat. To Stone, to the Lion's Den, even to El Jefe if someone industrious enough could make the connection. Somehow, that information could come to the attention of someone who could piece things together.

Bancroft was under orders to kill the boy to eliminate any possible chance of exposure. And since she was with him, that meant the woman, too.

But he'd never killed anyone before, least of all a child. The mandate weighed heavily on his shoulders and his conscience. Even though it meant incurring Stone's wrath and facing his own possible incarceration, Bancroft just couldn't do it. Couldn't kill even in psychological self-defense.

But someone was going to have to.

He pulled out his gun.

Her heart leaping into her throat, Tracy quickly pushed Jake behind her, shielding the small boy with her body. She glared defiantly at the policeman. "What is it you really want?"

Bancroft laughed at the irony of the question. "What I want is to get the hell away from everything that's gone wrong in my life. What I want is to go back and redo things, now that I know money isn't the solution to everything. It makes more problems than it solves." He'd turn a deaf ear to his wife's constant demands for more. She was like the fisherman's wife in the fairy tale, never satisfied, always wanting more. "What I want, Dr. Walker, is my life back the way it was before I joined the force." His expression sobered. "But we can't always have what we want." He took a deep breath. "I need you to get into the car I've got parked outside. Both of you."

Tracy made no move to comply. "Where are you taking us?"

"Some place other than here." Some place where someone else could come and do what he didn't have the stomach to do.

Tracy dug in. "No."

He stared at her. He was threatening her with a gun, he didn't expect her to pull this on him. Agitation fed the panic that was taking hold.

He cocked his gun. "Don't make me shoot you here, Doctor. I've suddenly become a very desperate man and desperate men do desperate things."

The wild look in his eyes subsided, giving way to one of pleading.

Her eyes held his. "You don't want to do this," Tracy said to him quietly, hoping to somehow convince him to give her the gun.

His fingers tightened around the hilt. "No, I don't. But I have no choice." He motioned toward the door with the barrel. "Please come with me."

She knew she had to play for time. Somehow, she had to get them out of this. "Can I get his jacket? It's cold outside."

He wasn't a monster, but he wasn't a fool either. "Where is it?"

"Right there." She pointed to the armchair.

As long as she wasn't out of sight, it was all right. Bancroft nodded. "Be quick about it."

As she picked up the jacket, something gleamed beneath it. Her nail file must have fallen out of her purse she realized. Palming it, she slipped the nail file into her pocket as she turned around with Jake's jacket. The boy was right behind her, closer than her shadow.

"It's okay, honey. We'll be all right." Kissing his cheek in an act of encouragement, she whispered against his ear. "Don't talk."

When she drew back, he looked at her as if he understood. She knew that if he talked, that would be the end of everything. Perhaps this way she could still convince the policeman that there was no reason to hold him.

Still on her knees, she looked up at the man. "All right, we're ready, but you're making a huge mistake."

He holstered his gun. "No, you made one by being here." Taking her hand, he hoisted her to her feet. Tracy stumbled and fell against him. She grabbed him as if to steady herself. Bancroft jerked away. "The next thing you try'll be the last."

"I tripped," she insisted. "Wait, his shoe is untied."

"Tie it," he ordered. This time, he stepped back toward the door.

Bending down, she quickly tightened Jake's shoe-
lace. And managed to leave the Lion's Den pin she
had palmed off Bancroft's lapel beside the chair on
the rug.

Chapter 14

The moment they were outside the door, Bancroft placed a restraining hand on Tracy's arm. It was as if he could read her thoughts. "If you try to get away, I shoot the boy first."

Bastard, her mind screamed. Glaring at Bancroft, she wound her arm protectively around Jake. "In front of all these witnesses?"

Bancroft quickly scanned the area. There were hardly any birds out, much less any people. The place was as dead as could be.

"What witnesses? This is the middle of the morning. Everyone's working." He motioned with his head, one hand covering the gun in his pocket. She had no doubt that it was pointed straight at the boy. And yet, there was something about the policeman, something that told her that he was trapped within this scenario as much as she and Jake were. "You see anybody?"

"No." *But Mrs. Wells, please see us,* she prayed. Tracy glanced toward the window across the way where she always saw the woman sitting, monitoring the comings and goings of everyone who lived within the complex. For the first time, the window was closed, the curtains were in place. Her heart sank.

The longer they stayed out here, the greater the chance that someone *would* come by. He motioned them to the squad car that was sitting in one of the many empty resident parking stalls.

"Now get into the car, both of you." As Jake started to climb into the back seat with Tracy, Bancroft pulled the boy over to him. "You sit up front with me," he told him sternly. He held the door open for Tracy who began to protest the separation. "You try anything..."

He didn't have to finish. It was the same threat as before. He would kill the boy.

Tracy sank her hands deep into her pockets. She could feel the nail file beneath her right hand. It was a puny weapon, but at least it was something and it comforted her.

"I won't try anything." *Not until Jake's out of the way,* she added silently. She got in, closing the door. Only then did Bancroft get in on his side. Jake cowered against the door, making his body as small as possible. She ached to comfort him. "Where are you taking us?"

"The only place I can."

The chief had an old cabin in the woods left to him

by his father. It was a place where he sometimes invited the inner circle of people who made up the Lion's Den. It gave everyone a chance to kick back, to bond. And to reinforce the notion that they were all interconnected. He knew where the key was kept. He'd bring the boy and woman there, Bancroft decided in desperation, and then turn the job over to Malloy. Malloy had made it clear that he no qualms about getting rid of anyone who got in his way.

Let this be on his conscience, Bancroft thought, starting up the car. He knew himself well enough to know that if he had to pull the trigger, he wouldn't.

But Stone was right. The boy couldn't be allowed to go free. Neither one of them could.

As the vehicle pulled away from the stall, Tracy twisted around in her seat, looking out the back window, willing Adam to return because he'd forgotten something, willing Mrs. Wells to come to her post at the window where she'd seen the older woman every single time before.

Neither happened.

Adam felt beat. There was no other word for it. He'd packed in a full day into less than four hours. There'd been two fires, one call coming in just as he'd entered the station, the other a little more than an hour before he left.

Both fires had been minor, the first at a residence, the second at an abandoned store, and both had been easily contained. But the adrenaline rush was always the same, whether for a minor fire or a major one because it took so little for the former to become the latter.

He supposed that the job was emotionally wearing on him.

Or maybe it was the emotions that were ricocheting through him ever since Tracy and Jake had come into his life that were taking their toll on him. Being with both of them stirred up so many memories, memories he swore to himself that he'd never retrieve again. Bittersweet memories of Gloria and Bobby and their life together that were painful to deal with.

But he had to in order to go forward. He hadn't thought he would actually do that, go forward. He figured that for the rest of his life, he would be sealed to one spot in time, a holding zone where he went neither forward or backward.

And then along came Tracy and suddenly all of his plans—or the lack of them—became moot. With her very presence, the woman pushed him forward. Pushing him into wanting more.

Pushing him into wanting what he once had. At times, it seemed as if what he was experiencing now was what he'd once had before. It was the same, and yet, it was different.

But with Tracy it would always be different, he thought, putting his key in the lock. Different in ways he hadn't even begun to comprehend.

The thought made him smile.

The first thing that assaulted him was the silence. Jake didn't talk, but Tracy did. For both of them. But there wasn't anything. Not Tracy, not the radio, or the television set or any combination of the three.

He tossed his keys onto the kitchen table and his jacket onto the armchair. The back of his mind registered that something was missing, but he wasn't sure what. Beyond the lack of noise.

"Hey, anyone want to greet a weary hero?" he called out. "I saved a cat today." He saw Tracy's pet nudging at something on his rug, or in it, given that the fabric was a short shag that had a tendency to swallow things like pet treats up. The sight of the animal was beginning to strike him as commonplace. Another milestone crossed, he mused, the corners of his mouth rising. "I know it's nothing like saving a pig, but we've all got to start somewhere." Adam paused to scratch the pig behind her ears. Petunia continued rooting. "Hi Petunia, where are they?"

Moving from area to area, it took Adam exactly fifteen seconds to ascertain that Petunia was the only one in the apartment.

That was odd, he thought. He could have sworn he saw Tracy's car parked in what was becoming her usual spot in guest parking. Crossing back to the door, he opened it and looked out.

The vehicle was still there.

Concern began to nudge at him. Adam shut the door, thinking.

If Tracy had gone out for a walk with Jake, she would have taken the pig with them. She was adamant about giving the animal as much exercise as she could, because of the erratic hours she'd been keeping lately. She never knew when she'd be around for the pet and it made her feel guilty to neglect the animal.

He looked down at the pet, who hadn't moved since he'd come in. "You know where she is?"

Shaking his head, Adam laughed to himself. Now she had him talking to a pig. The woman had turned his entire life on its ear and for some reason, it was bothering him less and less each day.

Petunia went into high gear, obviously after something she couldn't secure.

"Hey, hey, what are you doing? There are no truffles growing in my carpet. What are you digging at?" He knelt down to move the pig aside, away from whatever it was that had caught her fancy.

Something shiny embedded in the short shag strands flashed at him.

Picking it up, he stared at the item.

It was the pin he saw some of the policemen wearing. Flipping it over, he saw that the backing was missing, as if it'd caught on something and had been pulled off. Adam closed his hand over it. He knew this wasn't here this morning.

"Now what's this doing here?"

An uneasy feeling began to weave its way through him as he finally rose to his feet. The only people he'd seen wearing the pin, apart from that Brannigan woman who oversaw the Country Club, were policemen. Had any of them been here? Or was he just getting carried away?

Agitated, Adam stepped outside his door again, looking toward Tracy's spot, to make sure he hadn't just imagined her car being there.

He hadn't. It looked as if it hadn't moved since she'd arrived this morning.

Had the police come while he'd been at the fire station? But why? And why hadn't Tracy left him some kind of a note telling him where she'd be? She knew he was coming back early.

Adam turned, about to go back in to get his jacket and drive around the complex on the outside chance that she *had* gone for a walk. Who knew, maybe the pig had committed some kind of transgression and she was punishing her. With Tracy, he was never sure of anything.

Out of the corner of his eye, he saw Mrs. Wells trudging along, her arms wrapped around a large box. She was carrying it to the Dumpster located just beyond the block of mailboxes next to his door.

Releasing the doorknob, Adam quickly crossed to her. Maybe she'd seen Tracy leave with Jake. The woman prided herself on missing nothing.

"Here," he took the box from her, "let me take that for you."

Relieved, the small, squat woman blew out a breath. She beamed her thanks at him, the wrinkles on her face folding themselves over and over again.

"You're such a gentlemen, Mr. Collins. Not like some of the others around here." she looked accusingly over her shoulder at another apartment. "The old coot from 191 came out to get his newspaper and saw me struggling with this. Man just looked the other way." She snorted. "Probably too busy with that tart he's got in his apartment. Mind you—"

He normally let her rattle on while his mind drifted elsewhere, but he needed answers. "Mrs. Wells, did you happen to see a policeman earlier?"

She looked at him, happy to be able to impart the information he wanted. It was the first time he'd ever asked her anything.

Amanda Wells preened. "I surely did. He went in a little while after you left. Then he came out again about eight, ten minutes later. Took your lady friend and the boy with him." She raised her brows at him, requesting input. "Friend of yours?"

There was no one on the police force he was friends with, certainly no one who would come to his apartment. This didn't make any sense. "Not that I know of. What did he look like?"

She shook her head sadly. "Didn't get too good a look. The phone started ringing and it distracted me," she confessed, then proceeded to knock his socks off with the description she didn't think to be detailed. "Tall, thin, dirty blond hair cropped short like a soldier's, shoulders that looked as if they'd cave in at any minute." She paused, remembering. "Walked with a limp, I think."

The woman was a positive camera, he thought. She'd just described one of the two policemen who'd tried to question Jake in the hospital. If he'd come around to see if the boy was about to answer any questions yet, why would he take them to the police station? Jake couldn't talk. And even if he had taken them to the police station, why hadn't Tracy left a note to let him know?

Mrs. Wells stopped beside the enclosure that framed the Dumpster. It represented the complex management's attempt to keep the surroundings aesthetically pleasing. She cocked her head, peering at him as he tossed in her box.

"She in some kind of trouble, your lady friend?" The eager curiosity in her voice was unsuppressed.

God, I hope not. He dusted off his hands. "I guess I'll have to go down to the police station and find that out. Thanks for the information."

The round, almost elfin face sank into a deep frown as Adam began to walk away.

"Didn't look as if they were going to the police station," she called after him. "I had to answer the phone, but when I got back, I saw the squad car going in the opposite direction. West."

And the police station was directly east from here, he thought. Where the hell was the man going with them? Adam turned around to look at Mrs. Wells, something cold squeezing his heart. "West? There's nothing out there but the woods."

She thought for a moment. "Maybe he was taking them to the cabin."

"Cabin?"

Amanda Wells nodded, her beige-tinted hair fluttering in the breeze. "Chief's got a cabin out there. Has these big barbecues for all his men once or twice a year. Well, most of his men," she amended. She straightened a little before him, puffing up her more than ample chest. "My John and I used to go before he retired." And then she sighed forlornly. Her husband had been dead for a little more than two years. "Now, of course, I don't get to go anywhere any more—except to the Dumpster and back."

He ignored the dramatic performance and cut to the

heart of the matter. For reasons that were beyond him, something was horribly wrong and every minute might count. "Do you know where this cabin is?"

The smug smile was back. She knew what people said about her behind her back, that she was a gossip, a snoop, but that just wasn't so. She just liked knowing things. Nothing wrong with that. Look how eager the young fireman was to find out all she knew.

"Somewhere by the creek," she told him. "There are mountains in the background. You follow the road until it disappears. Have to leave the car some fifty yards away. The incline gets too steep." Finished, she sighed again. "Can't be any more specific than that."

It was a great deal more than he'd known a few minutes ago. Without Mrs. Wells, he wouldn't have known where to start, much less where to go. In a burst of enthusiasm that was completely foreign to him, he grasped the small woman by her shoulders and kissed her soundly on the mouth.

"Thanks, Mrs. Wells, I owe you more than you could possibly know."

Overwhelmed, she began to fan herself as she tried to refocus again. "But you'll tell me, right?" she asked eagerly. "Everything?"

"Every last blessed detail," he promised. "Just as soon as I get back."

She smiled to herself, running small, pudgy fingers over her lips.

Adam rushed back into his apartment to get his car keys from the kitchen table where he'd thrown them. He still had a lot of territory to cover, but at least he knew where to start.

Turning to grab his jacket, he nearly tripped over Petunia. Steadying himself, Adam looked down at the animal.

Petunia.

A thought suddenly came to him. Hell, it was just crazy enough to work.

"Okay, pig, Tracy says you can find her almost anywhere. We're going to play a really elaborate game of hide and seek. I promise if you find her, you never have to dig for another truffle again for the rest of your life."

Looking around, he saw the animal's leash on the back of one of the kitchen chairs. He picked it up and hooked the leash onto Petunia's collar. He would have felt a lot better if he'd had a bloodhound to depend on, but there wasn't time to try to round one up. The pig was going to have to do.

He went to the bedroom to retrieve something that belonged to Tracy.

Tracy's scalp tingled. Time was moving by as if in slow motion, despite the fact that they were going well over the speed limit. They had been ever since they'd left Mission Creek behind.

They were heading deep into the woods.

If the policeman meant to kill them and dump their bodies, no one was going to find them for a very long time. No one knew where they were.

What if Adam didn't find the pin she left? What if Petunia ate it? The pig didn't have a taste for metal, but that could change.

She upbraided herself for not grabbing Jake's hand

and trying to get away while they were still in the apartment complex. But the fear of having Jake hurt had stopped her. The look in his eyes had reflected sheer terror. She knew that he was counting on her to get him out of this.

If only she could.

"You don't have to do this," she told Bancroft. "Whatever you're involved in can't compare to what you're planning to do." She didn't want to say the word murder, afraid of upsetting Jake even more. But that was what this amounted to.

"You have no idea what I'm involved in," he snapped at her. Damn it, how had everything gotten so fouled up? "Look, for what it's worth, I'm sorry."

If he was sorry, if he was having any kind of regrets, maybe she could still get to him. "Then don't do anything to be sorry for."

"It's too late for that."

They were close. He knew the signs even though the cabin wasn't visible from here. They were going to have to leave the car as soon as the road ended.

Bancroft sighed, relieved. There was a phone at the cabin and he could call Malloy. His part in all this would be over with soon.

And then he was going to have to explain to Stone why he hadn't been the one to pull the trigger. He could feel his armpits sticking together with sweat despite the cold day. The chief didn't like anyone disobeying orders. Maybe Malloy could be bribed to keep his mouth shut.

He stopped the car.

Instantly alert, Tracy reached over the back of the

seat and grasped Jake's hand. The boy's fingers were like ice. He didn't need this. It wasn't fair. He'd already gone through so much more than a boy his age usually endured.

"Why are we stopping here?"

"To take in the view," Bancroft snapped. "Why the hell don't you stop asking so many questions?"

"I just want to know where we are."

"It's not going to make a difference to you." It wasn't his nature to terrorize women and children. What the hell had happened to him? He pushed back his hat and mopped the sweat from his brow with the back of his hand. "This is just a place I know. You'll have to stay here for a while."

A while. The phrase echoed in her head. Maybe he wasn't planning on killing them after all. Maybe this was some kind of elaborate kidnapping plot.

She looked at Jake. Once the matter of finances was settled and the red tape untangled, the boy was going to be worth a lot of money, far more than she surmised the policeman was destined to see in his lifetime.

Maybe Bancroft just wanted to ransom the boy. She clung to the thought. It bought them time.

"And then what?" she prodded.

His patience snapped. "Stop asking so many damn questions."

Getting out, his gun drawn, Bancroft hurried around the hood and grabbed Jake before Tracy had the opportunity to get the boy out of the squad car and make a run for it. He held the boy before him like a moving target.

"Walk," he ordered. "Get in front of me where I can see you."

"I don't know which way to go," she said innocently.

"Don't worry, I'll guide you."

Fear had a very real grip around her insides. With slow, precise steps, she began to walk. Patches of snow and ice pockmarked the area, cracking beneath her boots.

Adam drove his car as far as the road would allow him. Petunia was in the back, doing who knew what to his upholstery. He knew that anyone watching would have thought he'd lost his mind if they knew what he was attempting to do: track down a boy and a woman using a pig that had a fondness for both and a weakness for the truffles Tracy seemed to be endlessly producing out of her pocket.

Maybe he *had* lost his mind. He was expecting an order of pork loin on the hoof to act like Lassie.

Adam sighed. He didn't even know if Tracy and Jake were even out here. But he'd never known Mrs. Wells to be wrong. The woman was a human blotter for any and all information that came her way, retaining everything.

He made a mental note to take the older woman out on the town if he found Tracy and Jake.

When, he corrected adamantly. *When.*

Stopping the car, he got out and opened the rear door. Petunia jumped out far more daintily than her species warranted.

He picked up the strap winding it around his hand.

"This had better work," he told the potbellied pig. "Okay, find Tracy," he said, the way he had the last time Tracy had insisted on demonstrating the pig's abilities to him. Then she'd hidden in a closet. This place was a hell of a lot bigger than a closet.

Bending down, he held out Tracy's sweater in front of Petunia's snout.

To his undying amazement, the pig took off. Petunia seemed to know exactly what to do.

No one was ever going to believe this.

He didn't even know if he did. Holding on tightly to the leash, he followed the animal. Right past the squad car parked to the left of a heavily wooded area. A second one caught his eye, parked a little farther away.

Something was definitely wrong.

Adam recalled Mrs. Wells's description, that the cabin was some fifty yards ahead. But in which direction? Just then, Petunia pulled hard on her leash, squealing. She'd caught the scent of truffles, although he had no idea how.

And then he saw it.

The cabin. With the mountains behind it and a stream running not too far away from its location.

Stunned, Adam blessed all the strange beings who had come into his life to make this discovery possible.

Chapter 15

Adam made his way to the incline slowly, wishing he had brought a gun with him. But at least he had the element of surprise on his side, he consoled himself.

That, and a pig.

Somehow, he was going to have to figure out a way to use at least one of the two to his advantage. He looked around for some sort of a weapon to arm himself with. There were several broken branches lying on the ground, probably victims of the last electrical storm by the looks of some of the severed areas. He picked up one he felt he could swing hard.

It wasn't much, but then again, with the element of surprise working for him, it just might be enough.

The incline was even steeper than he'd thought. Mrs. Wells hadn't exaggerated. Worse than that, he'd be exposed, out in the open the entire way down.

All he could do was hope that whoever the squad cars belonged to weren't looking out the window when he came down. Once he was on flat ground again, there was a line of trees around the perimeter of the cabin. He could use those for cover until he was right at the cabin, ready to make his move.

Whatever that was going to be.

He looked at the pig. If he were to take a guess, he'd say she was going to have trouble going down.

"How surefooted are you? Or is that just for goats?" Petunia was still straining at the leash. He hoped that Tracy had been right about the pig being able to track her anywhere.

Deciding not to take a chance on having the pig slide and pull him all the way down to the bottom along with her, Adam picked Petunia up and started his descent. Mentally, he crossed his fingers.

There were two of them now. And whatever chance she thought she and Jake might have with Bancroft, Tracy knew no such chance existed with the second man. If the eyes were the windows to the soul, the man surely had none. His eyes were as dead as a raided tomb.

Nervous, her mind scrambling for a way out, Tracy was sitting on the chair where the policeman had ordered her to sit, holding Jake on her lap. Her arms were wrapped around him protectively.

The second man, wearing civilian clothes, had arrived only a few minutes ago and her blood had run cold when he'd looked at them.

Belatedly, she recognized him from the hospital.

He was the second policeman, the one who had leered at her. Who had gotten too incensed when she'd told them to leave.

This wasn't about kidnapping anymore, if it ever had been. This was about something far more deadly. They meant to kill them, here, in this two-story cabin that looked so cozy.

She thought of what Jake had told her just before the policeman had come to the apartment. This had to have something to do with what he'd seen at the country club. But what?

Tracy tried to make sense of what he'd said. Jake had told her that he'd seen some men dragging sacks out of the security room to a truck in the parking lot. What was it that they'd been dragging? Money? Things they'd stolen from the country club, or the members who frequented it? Maybe while the members were at the club, enjoying themselves, these men, whoever they were, went to their homes and stole things.

But that didn't make sense. Why bring the things to the club? And she hadn't heard of a rash of break-ins.

Maybe what had been in the bags was a body that had been cut up. No, that would have left a trail of blood that Jake would undoubtedly have noticed.

None of this was making any sense. What was in the bags? And who were the men Jake had seen?

She looked at her captors as they stood off to the side, talking, their voices low and menacing. Were these two men a part of whatever it was that Jake had seen? They obviously were afraid of what they thought he'd seen. Afraid that he could expose them. A cold shiver slid down her spine.

Afraid enough to kill.

Maybe they'd killed before. Maybe the bombing was somehow tied in to what they were doing, some kind of an elaborate cover-up that wound up killing two people and injuring fifteen others.

She was making herself crazy.

Tracy tightened her arms around Jake. It felt like he was trying to crawl right into her for shelter. For safety sake. She raised her head defiantly as she looked at the two men. "Why don't you let the boy go?"

Bancroft's nerves were frayed and close to breaking. "Why don't you shut up?" he snapped at her.

"She'll shut up soon enough," Malloy promised ominously, the grin on his lips making his face macabre. He stroked the hilt of the gun shoved into his waistband with his hand, his eyes slowly washing over Tracy.

Fear ripped into her, but anger was stronger. She sought refuge within it. Focusing on the policeman, she made her appeal to him. "Whatever you think, he isn't a threat to you. He can't talk. He's still traumatized from the bombing. I should know," she pleaded. "I'm his doctor."

Leaving Bancroft, Malloy crossed to her. His eyes gleamed as he began to mentally strip away her clothes. "Looks like you made a house call you shouldn't have, 'Doc.'"

There was an aura of evil in the room that was almost stifling. Tracy felt as if she was being stalked.

She looked to Bancroft. "You don't want a dead child on your conscience."

It had gone way past that. "I don't want a prison sentence, either."

"He is not a threat!" Tracy insisted heatedly. "Let him go." she forced herself to look at the other man. "Please."

Malloy stood over her, a powerful leg on either side of her legs. There was domination in his very countenance.

He was looming over her, stealing the air from her lungs, making Jake cower against her. "And what're you willing to do in exchange for that, 'Doc'?" Hands braced on either side of the chair, he leaned into her, so close that she could smell his breath. The stale smell of onions assaulted her nose. "Just how far are you willing to go, hmm?"

The sudden, unexpected pounding on the front door had them all stiffening.

The air was almost brittle with tension, just waiting for any excuse to shatter. Drawing his weapon, Malloy silently motioned for Bancroft to stand by the hostages. Changing places, Malloy crept to the door, then swung it open, his gun held chest high, ready to fire at any unwelcome target. When he saw nothing, he lowered his glance.

There was a pig standing in the doorway.

"What the hell—?" Stunned, Malloy looked past the threshold.

The next second, Adam exploded into the room, swinging the branch he'd picked up and connecting with Malloy's face. The man yelled with pain. Malloy's gun discharged as it flew out of his hand. Adam made a dive to the wooden floor and retrieved it. Malloy tried to pull him away. The two men were on the floor, fighting for final possession of the weapon.

The instant Tracy saw Petunia in the doorway, she knew Adam had found them. She pushed Jake off her lap and to the side, pulling out the nail file from her pocket. Holding the pointed metal like a weapon, she drove it into Bancroft's arm, twisting it as hard as she could.

The policeman screamed in rage and pain as blood spurted out of the wound. Tracy managed to pull Bancroft's revolver free of its holster. Grabbing Jake and pushing him behind her, she trained the weapon on the bleeding policeman.

"You move and I'll shoot you. I'm not much of a shot," she allowed, her voice vibrating with fury, "but at this range, I'm bound to hit something vital. I wouldn't risk it if I were you."

He wrapped his hand around his wound, pressing hard, trying to stem the bleeding. Desperate, he took a step toward her.

"You wouldn't—"

She cocked the trigger, aiming straight for his chest. She wouldn't get a second chance and she knew it. "Don't try me, mister. It's been a hell of a bad day so far."

The second gunshot had her jolting as she could feel its vibrations go straight through her as surely as if she'd been shot herself. Her eyes darted quickly to the side, praying that the shot hadn't gotten Adam. When she looked, she saw the other policeman slumped on the floor, blood beginning to flow and pool around his upper torso.

She felt tears stinging her eyes. That could have been Adam lying there. "You all right?" she asked hoarsely.

The branch was long gone from Adam's hand. In its place was the service revolver Malloy had initially dropped. The other man had been shot while grappling with Adam for it.

"I'm supposed to be asking you that," Adam pointed out. He was relieved beyond words that they were both all right. It had been one horrible close call. "You're one hell of a woman, you know that?"

The praise, so rare coming from him, warmed her. But even so, it was secondary to the relief she felt. He was alive. And they were all right. It could easily have gone the other way.

The pig waddled toward her on tiny, skittering feet. Tracy didn't want to risk the policeman snatching her and using the pet as a shield.

"Petunia, stay!" she ordered. The pig stopped as if it had turned to stone. Tracy looked at Bancroft. "In the sixties, they used to call the police pigs. Ironic isn't it?"

In response, Bancroft spat out a curse.

"Watch your mouth. There's a little boy present," Adam upbraided the man, taking him by the collar and shaking him. He looked toward the boy beside Tracy. "You all right, Jake?"

He nodded, his lower lip trembling. "Yes."

Adam's eyes widened as he looked at the boy. He'd

only expected a mute nod of the head. Was he imagining things? "Jake, you can talk!"

"This morning," Tracy told him. "Right after you left. I was going to call you, but then this one came to the apartment." She looked accusingly at Bancroft. "Jake said his first words after I recited the nursery rhyme, This Little Piggy to him."

Adam grinned at the animal on the floor. "You picked a hell of an amazing pet."

She smiled, looking at Petunia. Jake had dropped to his knees beside the pig and was hugging her for all he was worth. "Yes, didn't I? Okay, now what?"

"I handcuff our friend here." He took Bancroft's own handcuffs from his belt and, pulling the man's hands behind his back, flipped the cuffs onto Bancroft's wrists. "And call Chief Stone." Kneeling down beside the man on the floor, Adam felt for a pulse at his neck. There was none. "I suspect he'll want to talk to his man." His eyes slanted toward Bancroft. "I don't think I want to be in his shoes when the chief gets here."

Bancroft gave no indication that he'd heard, but he had. The pain in his arm seemed infinitely more preferable to what he knew lay ahead.

"Where are you going?" Adam asked as Tracy started to leave the room where she'd been held captive these past few hours.

"To find a bathroom and see if there're any bandages around. That wound needs to be tended before it gets infected."

"You'd tend him after he kidnapped you and Jake?" Adam asked incredulously.

"I'm a doctor first, an enraged woman second," she pointed out, leaving the room.

Adam shook his head. "Like I said, one hell of a woman."

Ben Stone liked to think that he gave the performance of his life. Like the good law enforcement officer he had once been, he came in with two of his most trusted men and asked for a brief summary of what had happened. He'd extended both courtesy and sympathy to Tracy and Jake for the ordeal they had gone through.

The only point he was adamant about was taking their statements before allowing the trio to go home.

"I need it now, while it's still fresh in your minds," Stone told them all. He was aware that his men were taking Malloy away in a body bag. He felt nothing. A man who couldn't do his job was of no use to him. Then he pointedly looked at Jake. "You understand that, don't you, son?"

Adam was holding the boy. Jake curved his body into him, as if to hide from the world. But the chief's gentle tone managed to soothe him and he nodded his head. "Uh-huh."

"Do you recognize either of these two men? Did you ever see them before?" he rephrased when the boy looked at him blankly. Jake nodded. The muscles in Stone's stomach tightened. Both men had been in the security room at the time the bomb had gone off. Was that where he recognized them from? "From where?" Stone prodded, deliberately keeping his voice on a low keel.

"The hospital. They came to ask me questions,'' Jake remembered.

Stone studied the small, thin face. The Anderson boy was too young to be deceptive. Maybe the trauma of the bombing had knocked everything else from his mind. Which was fine with him. Trouble was, he still wasn't sure this wouldn't come back and bite him on his butt at some later date.

"Okay, Champ,'' Stone said to Jake. "See, you just answered my question. That wasn't so hard, now was it?''

Jake shook his head and then buried it further into Adam's chest.

Stone patted Jake's head. "You know, I don't think there's anything to be gained by making you give those statements tonight. Why don't you good folks go home and stop by the station tomorrow morning? You can give your statements then. You've all been through a lot today.''

Tracy nodded, relieved for the reprieve. "Thank you, Chief. That's awfully decent of you.''

Stone's smile was almost beatific. "Haven't you heard? I'm a decent kind of guy just trying to do his job the best way he knows how.''

He glanced toward Bancroft. Not only had the man bungled the job he'd sent him out to do, but he'd gotten another member of their group killed. A man like that was the type to turn state's evidence. He'd never trusted a man with a conscience.

Wheels began to turn in his head. Maybe he could turn this to his advantage somehow, maybe even pin the bombing on Bancroft. But that would require a certain degree of alteration to the situation. Stone's frown was deep. "Even if I do seem to have rogue cops working for me," he concluded.

"You can't be responsible for everybody," Adam assured him. No man or woman could spread themselves that thin.

"But it's my job to be," Stone corrected. He tipped his hat to Tracy and nodded at Adam and the boy. "Sometime tomorrow morning," he repeated. He motioned to one of the two men in the room. "I'll have Officer Evans drive you home."

"No need," Adam assured him quickly. He didn't want anyone coming home with them. He'd done some soul searching these past few hours and he wanted a quiet arena when they returned to his apartment. "You've got your hands full and I've got my car parked on the ridge."

Stone nodded. There was no reason to press the issue. He was fairly confident that the boy knew nothing and if he didn't, the people he remained with certainly didn't.

"Well, goodnight then." Turning on his heel, Stone went to deal with the man who had so sorely disappointed him.

Tracy walked into the living room to find Adam sitting there, a strange solemn expression on his face. She was exhausted beyond human measurement. She was definitely too tired to deal with anything else, she thought, dropping onto the sofa with a huge sigh.

Adam looked her way, shifting as he raised a brow. "He asleep?"

She nodded. "Finally. He was dog tired, but too tense to close his eyes." She'd left Petunia with Jake, referring to the animal as a guard pig. Jake had giggled. The pig was now draped across his feet. "You know, it's going to be a while before he feels safe again." And then she smiled. "Although having a hero around to watch over him will help."

"You referring to me or the pig."

She fought the temptation to say both. "You."

He laughed. "You weren't exactly a slouch yourself. What did you stab that policemen with, anyway?" In all the excitement, he'd forgotten to ask.

"A nail file." He looked at her in complete surprise. "I grabbed it when I got Jake's jacket."

Adam sat down beside her, slipping an arm around her shoulders. He drew her closer to him. "You really are amazing."

She snuggled against him, thinking how nice that felt. To have a man in her life. To love him. "Go on. You have my attention."

He picked at words carefully, stringing them together. "And I was sitting here, thinking…"

She could feel her heart speed up again. Was this going to be good, or bad? "About?"

The emotion in his voice was restrained with tight, steely bands but it still managed to get through. "About how it felt when I came home and found that you weren't here. How it felt when I thought you were in trouble."

She could feel herself taking that first tentative step on the tightrope. But she had to ask. "And how did it feel?"

Adam rested his head on top of her head. It felt so good to have her against him like this. He never wanted to move from this spot. "Like I was never so scared in my whole life."

Her soft laugh lilted in the air. "Coming from a firefighter, that's some declaration."

Drawing back, he looked at her. "I'm serious. It made me realize something."

She could feel herself bracing for the shoe to fall. "What?"

This was hard for him. Words had never come easily. But she deserved to know what was in his heart. "That I don't want to be without you. That my life would be empty without you."

She rested her hand on his chest. She could feel his heart beating beneath her fingertips. The rhythm was comforting. "I'm not going anywhere."

"But I want you to."

She stiffened. He'd managed to hit her squarely between the eyes, she thought. And she had just stood there, like some stupid target. She'd been through a hell of a lot today and the normally long fuse she had had been shortened considerably.

Her temper flared. "Is this about asking me to back away, about loving being too difficult for you, because if it is—"

"It's about asking you to marry me," he blurted out the words, talking over her. He hadn't meant to do it this way, but now that it was out, he was relieved.

"—I can't just cut bait and—" His words suddenly

hit. Her eyes widened as she stared at him. "What did you just say?"

He let out a deep breath. Once was hard enough, twice he might not get through it. Wasn't she listening? "I'm proposing."

Her eyes narrowed. She had to be making a mistake. "To who?"

The laugh was tinged in nervousness. Was she stalling just to turn him down? "Petunia's not my type, so I guess it's to you."

Alarms went off throughout her body as tears threatened to form. "Don't kid about things like that—"

"I'm not," he insisted. Shifting, he took her hands in his and looked into her eyes. Trying to convince her. "I love you, Tracy. I didn't want to, didn't want to admit it when I knew, but there's no getting around it. I love you and I want you in my life permanently."

She immediately thought of the reason that she had drawn back from every man who had tried to pay attention to her ever since she'd been diagnosed. "But I can't give you children—"

He shook his head. She was wrong. "You already gave me one—Jake. He's crazy about you and he seems to like me. We can adopt him. And if that's not enough for you, we can adopt more. It's not genes that make a child your own, it's love." He knew she knew he was making sense. "And you and Jake have shown me that I still can love." When she said nothing, he took it to mean that he'd misread the signs. That she didn't feel the same way about him as he did about her. He backed up emotionally. "I'm sorry, I didn't mean to sound like I'm rushing you—"

"Rush me. I've waited thirty years for this. Rush me." She threw her arms around his neck. "I love you, Adam Collins and I would love nothing more than to be your wife." Her eyes sparkled. "End of story."

"No, I've got a hunch it's just the beginning."

She grinned just before he kissed her. "Maybe you're right at that."

Epilogue

Bancroft cowered in the holding cell where he'd been placed. The chief hadn't said a single word to him, not at the cabin after he'd arrived with two of his men and read him his rights. And not since they'd reached the police station. It was like standing on the edge of a volcano, waiting for it to erupt.

Once at the station, he'd found himself being roughly escorted into the holding cell by men he'd counted among his friends.

Men who didn't utter a word in response to the nervous questions he fired at them. They'd merely looked past him, as if he didn't exist.

As if he were already a ghost in their lives.

He'd been placed in the holding cell that was separated from the rest of the cells by a corridor and a wall. This was where they placed prisoners whose interrogation would not stand up to close scrutiny.

This was where things happened that no one talked about.

It didn't always used to be that way, Bancroft tried to console himself. Once this had been the cell where the town drunks had slept off their inebriation, to be released in the morning. Maybe the two policemen, Evans and Neely, had just put him in here so that nobody had to see a—what was it Stone had called him? A rogue cop. That was it. Maybe they'd done it so he could retain a little of his dignity.

The silence was unnerving him.

His palms were sweating as he rubbed them against each other and his stomach was so knotted he was having trouble drawing in air. He'd been fingerprinted like a common criminal, his belt and shoelaces taken away from him along with the things in his pockets. The only one who had even looked at him as if he was something other than dirt when he'd been herded through the station to the cell was that female cop, Molly something.

No, that wasn't right, he amended. Some of the cops had looked at him with apprehension. Like they thought he'd talk if pressed.

Maybe he would, he thought, scrambling to find something to hold on to. Maybe that was his bargaining chip. He'd tell Stone that he wouldn't talk to the higher authorities about what was going on in the back room at the Lone Star Country Club if the chief would just turn his back and let him go free. He'd leave everything behind and get the hell out of this place. The money, they could have that, they could have everything. He didn't care about anything anymore.

All he wanted was his freedom.

The cell was cold. His shirt was sticking to his back.

The sound of approaching footsteps had him jerking his head up, straining to hear. On his feet again, Bancroft wrapped his hands around the bars, craning his neck to try to see who was coming.

The figure came into view.

It was all or nothing, Bancroft thought. "Oh, it's you. Good. I have something to say."

Stone searched his pockets for a match. He'd left his damn lighter someplace again and he needed a smoke. Badly. This powder keg he was sitting on kept defying containment. He didn't like that.

He should have known that if you wanted a thing done right, you did it yourself. The more people you trusted, the greater the risk became. Weak links always cropped up and there were weak links in this chain....

The urgent knock on his door interrupted his search. The next second, the door to his office was being opened and one of the new men, Mulrooney, burst in.

Stone looked at him coldly before lowering his eyes to the center desk drawer he'd just opened. "When you knock, you're supposed to wait for a response."

"I'm sorry, Chief, but you're going to want to come quick to see this."

Stone closed the drawer. There were no matches there. "See what?"

"It's Bancroft—"

The chief raised a brow. "What about him?"

"French went to see him and then she came right out again, yelling for me to come with her and—" Mulrooney licked his lips, the horror of the scene freshly imprinted on his mind. He was still a rookie and hadn't seen death close-up yet. Until now.

"And?"

"He hung himself, Chief. With his belt. I found him just hanging there like a side of beef—" Mulrooney's voice almost broke.

Stone shook his head. "Poor bastard." He sighed heavily. "Look, I'll be right there. If you haven't yet, get some men to cut him down. I've just got to finish something first."

Numbly, Mulrooney nodded, withdrawing.

"And shut the door, will you?"

"Yes, sir."

Stone waited until the door was closed. Finding a half-used matchbook in the top side drawer, he settled back in his chair and lit the cigar he'd been saving.

One loose end down.

*   *   *   *   *

Be sure to look for
the next exciting book in the
LONE STAR COUNTRY CLUB *series,*
IN THE LINE OF FIRE,
by Beverly Bird,
available in March 2002,
only from Silhouette Intimate Moments.

Chapter 1

It was raining hard in south Texas.

It wasn't the general impotent misting that he'd come to accept as a squall during his formative years in Mission Creek, Danny Gates thought as he stood on the concrete sidewalk of Main Street for the first time in six years. *That* sort of rain would have been a kind of "welcome home, boy." This rain was rude and punishing. It slid down the back of his neck, a cold finger trailing memories, most of them of the freedom he'd enjoyed years ago.

He started to pull up the collar of his jacket, then he remembered, too, that he no longer owned one. He'd been dragged off to jail without warning on a blisteringly hot July afternoon. He'd been denied the bail that would have allowed him a window of time to get his affairs in order. As a result, almost everything he'd owned back then was just...gone now.

Danny took a step off the curb. A glaring yellow
taxi pushed toward him through hardy traffic and he
started to wave it down. He aborted the gesture just
in time to shove his hand into his jeans pocket and
pull out a few crinkled bills. He had six dollars and
some change left of the money that the state of Texas
had given him as a parting gift. Not enough for cab
fare to his mother's home out on the poor end of Gulf
Road, not even six years ago.

Danny swore aloud. His brown eyes darkened dangerously in the direction of the driver as the car approached. His expression obviously warned the cab-
bie that he didn't want to pick this man up after all
because the yellow car sped on.

He'd have to work on that, Danny thought, rubbing
a hand over his jaw as though to erase the expression.

He started walking, turning off Main Street, leaving
Lone Star County's Probation Offices behind. He
didn't even dare stick his thumb out as he would have
done as a kid. Hitchhiking was considered a minor
crime in most societies, and Danny suspected that
Mission Creek was probably one of them. Any ridic-
ulous infraction now could get his parole revoked.

He was an ex-mobster, and an ex-con. He accepted
responsibility for the first if not the second. He
trudged on, toward whatever fate had in store for him
in this second chance at life.

Silhouette®

I N T I M A T E   M O M E N T S™

 LONE STAR LSCC **COUNTRY CLUB** EST. 1923

Where Texas society reigns supreme—and appearances are everything!

When a bomb rips through the historic Lone Star Country Club, a mystery begins in Mission Creek....

Available February 2002
ONCE A FATHER (IM #1132)
by Marie Ferrarella
A lonely firefighter and a warmhearted doctor fall in love while trying to help a five-year-old boy orphaned by the bombing.

Available March 2002
IN THE LINE OF FIRE (IM #1138)
by Beverly Bird
Can a lady cop on the bombing task force and a sexy ex-con stop fighting long enough to realize they're crazy about each other?

Available April 2002
MOMENT OF TRUTH (IM #1143)
by Maggie Price
A bomb tech returns home to Mission Creek and discovers that an old flame has been keeping a secret from him....

And be sure not to miss the Silhouette anthology

Lone Star Country Club: The Debutantes

Available in May 2002

Available at your favorite retail outlet.

 Silhouette®
Where love comes alive™

Uncover the truth behind

CODE NAME: DANGER

in **Merline Lovelace's** thrilling duo

DANGEROUS TO HOLD

When tricky situations need a cool head, quick wits and a touch of ruthlessness, Adam Ridgeway, director of the top secret OMEGA agency, sends in his team. Lately, though, his agents have had romantic troubles of their own....

NIGHT OF THE JAGUAR
&
THE COWBOY AND THE COSSACK

And don't miss
HOT AS ICE (IM #1129, 2/02)
which features the newest OMEGA adventure!

DANGEROUS TO HOLD is available this February
at your local retail outlet!

Look for ***DANGEROUS TO KNOW,*** the second set of
stories in this collection, in July 2002.

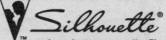
Where love comes alive™

This Mother's Day
Give Your Mom
🌸 A Royal Treat 🌸

Win a fabulous one-week vacation in
Puerto Rico for you and your mother at
the luxurious Inter-Continental San Juan
Resort & Casino. The prize includes round
trip airfare for two, breakfast daily and a
mother and daughter day of beauty
at the beachfront hotel's spa.

⬢

INTER·CONTINENTAL
San Juan
RESORT & CASINO

Here's all you have to do:

Tell us in 100 words or less how your
mother helped with the romance in your
life. It may be a story about your engagement,
wedding or those boyfriends when you were
a teenager or any other romantic advice
from your mother. The entry will be judged
based on its originality, emotionally
compelling nature and sincerity.
See official rules on following page.

Send your entry to:
Mother's Day Contest

In Canada	**In U.S.A.**
P.O. Box 637	P.O. Box 9076
Fort Erie, Ontario	3010 Walden Ave.
L2A 5X3	Buffalo, NY
	14269-9076

Or enter online at www.eHarlequin.com

All entries must be postmarked by April 1, 2002.
Winner will be announced May 1, 2002. Contest open to
Canadian and U.S. residents who are 18 years of age and older.
No purchase necessary to enter. Void where prohibited.

PRROY

Two ways to enter:

• **Via The Internet:** Log on to the Harlequin romance website (www.eHarlequin.com) anytime beginning 12:01 a.m. E.S.T., January 1, 2002 through 11:59 p.m. E.S.T., April 1, 2002 and follow the directions displayed on-line to enter your name, address (including zip code), e-mail address and in 100 words or fewer, describe how your mother helped with the romance in your life.

• **Via Mail:** Handprint (or type) on an 8 1/2" x 11" plain piece of paper, your name, address (including zip code) and e-mail address (if you have one), and in 100 words or fewer, describe how your mother helped with the romance in your life. Mail your entry via first-class mail to: Harlequin Mother's Day Contest 2216, (in the U.S.) P.O. Box 9076, Buffalo, NY 14269-9076; (in Canada) P.O. Box 637, Fort Erie, Ontario, Canada L2A 5X3.

For eligibility, entries must be submitted either through a completed Internet transmission or postmarked no later than 11:59 p.m. E.S.T., April 1, 2002 (mail-in entries must be received by April 9, 2002). Limit one entry per person, household address and e-mail address. On-line and/or mailed entries received from persons residing in geographic areas in which entry is not permissible will be disqualified.

Entries will be judged by a panel of judges, consisting of members of the Harlequin editorial, marketing and public relations staff using the following criteria:
> • Originality - 50%
> • Emotional Appeal - 25%
> • Sincerity - 25%

In the event of a tie, duplicate prizes will be awarded. Decisions of the judges are final.

Prize: A 6-night/7-day stay for two at the Inter-Continental San Juan Resort & Casino, including round-trip coach air transportation from gateway airport nearest winner's home (approximate retail value: $4,000). Prize includes breakfast daily and a mother and daughter day of beauty at the beachfront hotel's spa. Prize consists of only those items listed as part of the prize. Prize is valued in U.S. currency.

All entries become the property of Torstar Corp. and will not be returned. No responsibility is assumed for lost, late, illegible, incomplete, inaccurate, non-delivered or misdirected mail or misdirected e-mail, for technical, hardware or software failures of any kind, lost or unavailable network connections, or failed, incomplete, garbled or delayed computer transmission or any human error which may occur in the receipt or processing of the entries in this Contest.

Contest open only to residents of the U.S. (except Colorado) and Canada, who are 18 years of age or older and is void wherever prohibited by law; all applicable laws and regulations apply. Any litigation within the Province of Quebec respecting the conduct or organization of a publicity contest may be submitted to the Régie des alcools, des courses et des jeux for a ruling. Any litigation respecting the awarding of a prize may be submitted to the Régie des alcools, des courses et des jeux only for the purpose of helping the parties reach a settlement. Employees and immediate family members of Torstar Corp. and D.L. Blair, Inc., their affiliates, subsidiaries and all other agencies, entities and persons connected with the development, marketing or conduct of this Contest are not eligible to enter. Taxes on prize are the sole responsibility of winner. Acceptance of any prize offered constitutes permission to use winner's name, photograph or other likeness for the purposes of advertising, trade and promotion on behalf of Torstar Corp., its affiliates and subsidiaries without further compensation to the winner, unless prohibited by law.

Winner will be determined no later than April 15, 2002 and be notified by mail. Winner will be required to sign and return an Affidavit of Eligibility form within 15 days after winner notification. Non-compliance within that time period may result in disqualification and an alternate winner may be selected. Winner of trip must execute a Release of Liability prior to ticketing and must possess required travel documents (e.g. Passport, photo ID) where applicable. Travel must be completed within 12 months of selection and is subject to traveling companion completing and returning a Release of Liability prior to travel; and hotel and flight accommodations availability. Certain restrictions and blackout dates may apply. No substitution of prize permitted by winner. Torstar Corp. and D.L. Blair, Inc., their parents, affiliates, and subsidiaries are not responsible for errors in printing or electronic presentation of Contest, or entries. In the event of printing or other errors which may result in unintended prize values or duplication of prizes, all affected entries shall be null and void. If for any reason the Internet portion of the Contest is not capable of running as planned, including infection by computer virus, bugs, tampering, unauthorized intervention, fraud, technical failures, or any other causes beyond the control of Torstar Corp. which corrupt or affect the administration, secrecy, fairness, integrity or proper conduct of the Contest, Torstar Corp. reserves the right, at its sole discretion, to disqualify any individual who tampers with the entry process and to cancel, terminate, modify or suspend the Contest or the Internet portion thereof. In the event the Internet portion must be terminated a notice will be posted on the website and all entries received prior to termination will be judged in accordance with these rules. In the event of a dispute regarding an on-line entry, the entry will be deemed submitted by the authorized holder of the e-mail account submitted at the time of entry. Authorized account holder is defined as the natural person who is assigned to an e-mail address by an Internet access provider, on-line service provider or other organization that is responsible for arranging e-mail address for the domain associated with the submitted e-mail address. Torstar Corp. and/or D.L. Blair Inc. assumes no responsibility for any computer injury or damage related to or resulting from accessing and/or downloading any sweepstakes material. Rules are subject to any requirements/limitations imposed by the FCC. Purchase or acceptance of a product offer does not improve your chances of winning.

For winner's name (available after May 1, 2002), send a self-addressed, stamped envelope to: Harlequin Mother's Day Contest Winners 2216, P.O. Box 4200 Blair, NE 68009-4200 or you may access the www.eHarlequin.com Web site through June 3, 2002.

Contest sponsored by Torstar Corp., P.O. Box 9042, Buffalo, NY 14269-9042.

 *Silhouette*®

where love comes alive—online...

eHARLEQUIN.com

your romantic magazine

—Indulgences—

♥ Monthly guides to indulging yourself, such as:
 ★ Tub Time: A guide for bathing beauties
 ★ Magic Massages: A treat for tired feet

—Horoscopes—

♥ Find your daily Passionscope, weekly Lovescopes and Erotiscopes

♥ Try our compatibility game

—Romantic Movies—

♥ Read all the latest romantic movie reviews

—Royal Romance—

♥ Get the latest scoop on your favorite royal romances

—Romantic Travel—

♥ For the most romantic destinations, hotels and travel activities

All this and more available at
www.eHarlequin.com